# A Vow from a Viscount

## Vows in Vauxhall Gardens, Book 3

## Daphne Quinn

## ARE YOU SIGNED UP FOR DRAGONBLADE'S BLOG?

You'll get the latest news and information on exclusive giveaways, exclusive excerpts, coming releases, sales, free books, cover reveals and more.

Check out our complete list of authors, too!

No spam, no junk. That's a promise!

### Sign Up Here

www.dragonbladepublishing.com

*Dearest Reader;*

*Thank you for your support of a small press. At Dragonblade Publishing, we strive to bring you the highest quality Historical Romance from some of the best authors in the business. Without your support, there is no 'us', so we sincerely hope you adore these stories and find some new favorite authors along the way.*

*Happy Reading!*

*CEO, Dragonblade Publishing*

# Additional Dragonblade books by Author Daphne Quinn

**Vows in Vauxhall Gardens**
The Lady of the Lamps (Book 1)
Entertaining the Earl (Book 2)
A Vow from a Viscount (Book 3)

# CHAPTER ONE

"Is that Laurence Walsham?" The words were whispered behind fans by giggling débutantes and scandalized matrons as Laurence strode through the hall, pretending not to hear his name on their lips.

He tipped a wink at a lady dressed in a green gown, her red hair piled high upon her head. Her cheeks flushed scarlet, and her companions immediately looked at her with wide eyes.

They obviously thought she was the latest of his paramours—although, in truth, he had never met the lady before. He just rather liked redheads and how easy it generally seemed to be to make them blush.

He planned to enjoy a dance or two, a chance to see what exquisite ladies were present at this point in the season, and then retire to the cardroom. He was sure he had spotted more than one fellow he knew from his days at Eton, so it would be a pleasant evening. Then, he thought, he might go on to visit Lady Astley, who was his actual latest paramour—although, somehow, her name had so far stayed out of the gossip columns.

Not that he thought she'd be overly bothered. She was a widow twice over and had no wish to remarry. Her reputation was not so important to her these days.

He reached the refreshment table and took a glass of wine before turning to survey the room. It was busy, despite the season drawing to a close. One last hurrah, he supposed, before everyone disappeared to the country for hunting and other such genteel pursuits.

Laurence enjoyed the city, but he would return to his family estate to see his father, Viscount Walsham. Perhaps unusual for fathers and sons within the ton, they enjoyed one another's company—although his father no longer wished to return to the city every year for the season. He only occasionally attended Parliament if the vote was particularly important. With no plans to take a second wife, he said there was no point in returning for the whole season every year.

He did not like to hear that Laurence had no current plans to take a wife either, yet still found London and the season most enjoyable.

"Walsham?" Laurence turned at the sound of his name, spoken directly instead of whispered behind a fan, and found himself face-to-face with Henry Cassel, a classmate from his school days.

"I thought it was you. How are you, old friend?"

Laurence raised his glass with an easy smile. "I cannot complain. And you? The last I heard, you were touring the Continent."

"I was—I returned in the spring with my wife, Emily. And I cannot complain either, thank you."

"I had not heard that you had married. Congratulations," he said, raising his glass once more and then draining it. His friend seemed happy, and it clearly was not the time to give his own views on marriage. It wasn't that he thought it was a bad thing, just that he was not sure whether two people were really meant to spend their entire lives together. People grew and changed— did that not mean it was better to move on and find someone with whom you had things in common?

Laurence's acquaintances rarely lasted an entire season—and that was fine by him. But he did not think those were words to say to a man newlywed and clearly happy about it.

"Thank you. We met and married in France, so no one really knew until we returned. And I presume, considering the amount of gossip I heard when you walked into the room, that you are not yet wed?"

Laurence laughed. "You should know better than to listen to gossip, Henry."

"You cannot be oblivious to the fact that your name ripples around the room as soon as you enter," Henry said with a raised eyebrow. "And that the words 'rake' and 'ruinous' seem to follow you."

Laurence let out a huff. "*Rake* I'll accept. *Ruinous* is unfair and unfounded."

Henry laughed. "Understood."

"You are right, I have not married yet."

"I suppose we are still young," Henry said with a smile. "One day, the viscountcy will surely need an heir…"

Laurence felt his jaw stiffen at the topic. Of course, it was an undeniable truth that one day he would need to wed and produce an heir. But he did not like to think of that day—because he did not wish to contemplate his father dying and leaving him as the viscount. And he did not like to ruminate on the promise he had made his father… A promise that would certainly require him to change the way he had been living his life for the past few years.

And he very much enjoyed his life. He liked flirting, he liked dancing, he liked knowing that the women he spent time with were happy and content and knew there would be no offer of marriage forthcoming.

He didn't want things to change… But even a future viscount had no power to stop the future from coming.

"All in good time," he said in the end, reaching for another glass. "You must introduce me to your lovely wife, Henry. And we must have dinner sometime. It has been too long since I last saw you."

Henry smiled. "Indeed. Perhaps I'll see you at the faro table later—if you can tear yourself away from the lovely ladies in here."

MISS ANASTASIA CARRINGTON felt decidedly awkward in the ballroom, standing at the edge of the dance floor, completely alone.

She did not feel ready to be out enjoying such gaiety. However, her brother had insisted that it was time for them to cast aside their mourning clothes and re-enter society. She didn't want to be there, but Oliver had made it clear she needed to find a husband.

She had not expected him to disappear almost as soon as they arrived. This was her first ton event since her father had passed. She was not well acquainted with anyone. She had no older female to guide her through society, with their mother having died many years earlier. And apparently, her brother did not plan to keep her company or instruct her in the ways of such gatherings. So she stood at the edge, feeling shy and unsure, wishing desperately for a mother, sisters, or friends... Some camaraderie with whom to enter this fray.

Anastasia hugged her arms around her waist and found herself wishing she could disappear. Although, she thought, perhaps she was already rather invisible to the crowd. While her red hair and blue eyes were often commented upon, her petite stature and the fact that she was alone meant that she did not attract much attention.

And she didn't want to. She didn't want to be here. But she could not go home without Oliver. And who knew how late he would want to stay? Once he had a drink or two and sat down at the card table... Well, it was hard to pry him away.

She watched the couples dancing, intricate steps that she knew by heart from her hours with the dance master. Not that she'd had much opportunity to put those skills into practice. With her father passing away so soon after she had first made her debut in society, there had been no cause—nor any desire—to dance.

But she had not forgotten those skills. She rather thought it was like when one learned to ride a horse…even if you did not ride again for several months, you did not forget how to do so.

"Not dancing, Annie?" a loud voice called, and she was startled to turn and find her brother ambling toward her, his eyes bright and his cheeks red. He only called her *Annie* when he was in his cups, and that was the only time he smiled like that, too.

He had barely spoken to her since Papa had died, other than to bark orders. So this friendliness was a welcome change—even if he was clearly drunk.

Although she did not wish for him to attract so much attention with his loud words.

He was carrying a glass of wine—only the one, he would never have thought of getting his sister some refreshment—although its contents had mostly been drunk.

"No," Anastasia said softly. "No one has asked me."

Oliver harrumphed. "Well, you don't exactly look like you want to, do you? Standing there with your arms wrapped around your stomach and your shoulders slumped. The gentlemen will think you're sickening for something."

Anastasia felt her cheeks flush red, something that happened all too frequently, and she let her arms drop down by her sides, embarrassed that her brother already found her wanting in such a social situation.

"You cannot be a burden forever, sister. You must find a husband—you know that."

"Yes, brother," she said with a nod. She didn't feel that Oliver was being entirely fair, but she knew better than to argue with him. She had heard that redheads were famed for their tempers, and while she did not think it true of herself, it certainly was for Oliver Carrington.

She wanted to marry, and she would ensure that she did everything she could to find herself a husband who would make both her and her brother happy. But it wasn't as if she had been out in society for years and years without an offer.

This was her first night back in society—could she really be criticized for not yet having found a husband?

She drew her shoulders back and tried to portray a confidence she did not feel. At least if a gentleman asked her to dance, her brother might be more pleased with her conduct.

"Goodness me," Oliver said, waving his wine glass in the air so exuberantly that several drops of the ruby liquid spilled onto the floor. "Walsham! Is that you?"

A tall, lean gentleman with dark hair tied back with a red velvet ribbon, paused and turned his head. He had an angular face, and yet his brown eyes were warm, almost in contrast.

"Mr. Carrington," the man said, "what a pleasure to see you again."

"The pleasure is mine, Mr. Walsham," Oliver said with a bow of his head.

The man's eyes flickered in Anastasia's direction, and Oliver clearly remembered that she was there.

"Please, allow me to present my sister, Miss Anastasia Carrington. This is Mr. Walsham—we met at White's last year."

Anastasia curtsied to the handsome gentleman before her. He nodded his head in return, a smile playing on his lips.

"A pleasure to meet you, Miss Carrington. I do not remember seeing you at any of the events this season."

He gave her a look that suggested he would remember if he had seen her, and it made her stomach feel rather strange.

"My father passed away," Anastasia said by way of explanation.

His appraising gaze softened. "I am sorry to hear that. I can only imagine how difficult such a loss would be."

"Thank you," Anastasia said, holding his gaze.

Oliver mumbled something that sounded rather like, *At least you'll get a viscountcy when your father passes.* Anastasia could not quite believe that her brother could be so callous, even in his cups—and she hoped that Mr. Walsham had not heard him.

"Are you enjoying your evening, Mr. Walsham?" she asked,

hoping to cover the blunder.

"I am, thank you. And if you would give me the honor of the next dance, I believe I would enjoy it even more."

# CHAPTER TWO

ALTHOUGH SHE HAD spent the evening waiting to be asked to dance, when it finally happened, she found herself at a loss for words.

He was just so handsome. Tall, imposing, with dark eyes that made her feel like she might melt into a puddle before him.

"Yes, Mr. Walsham. Of course," she managed to say eventually, just catching a look of irritation on her brother's face that she did not fully understand. Surely he would be pleased that she had been asked to dance? Especially by the son of a viscount—and one he apparently knew, too.

As the musicians prepared for the next dance, the gentleman offered his hand to her and led her onto the dance floor.

He bowed to her, and she curtsied back, and they danced in near silence until he said, "Allow me to say what an enchanting shade of red your hair is, Miss Carrington. Why, under the light of the candles, it almost looks like flames."

Anastasia couldn't help but smile. She found her red hair often attracted attention, but more for being unusual—something that marked her as different—rather than something that was generally complimented. She had always liked its rich shade, especially as it was so similar to their dearly departed mother's, but she did not think that was the common consensus.

"You are very kind, sir."

"Not kind," he said when the dance brought them back together, "Merely honest. I must tell a beautiful woman she is beautiful if I have the chance."

Anastasia found herself blushing and could not meet his eye. She did not think she had ever been called beautiful before—and certainly not by a man as handsome as Mr. Walsham.

They did not speak again, and when the dance came to a close, he bowed low before her and said, "Your servant," before leading her back to her brother, who had—rather surprisingly—remained to watch the entire dance.

As she stood and watched the people milling around, her eyes were drawn to Mr. Walsham's tall figure as he cut through the crowd, perhaps on his way to procure refreshment or to ask another young lady to dance.

She could not tear her eyes from him.

"I have a card game starting soon. Once it is over, we shall leave."

"Very well, Oliver." It was not a case of when the card game ended, but when her brother ran out of money. She knew little of matters of the estate, and yet she knew they had never had to worry about money while Papa had been alive. At the rate Oliver had been spending since his death… she hoped there was no need for concern. She didn't dare mention the amount of money she knew Oliver was spending on drinking, gambling, and other pursuits.

It wasn't her place. He owned everything—and she was a burden.

That was the way of the world. She just hoped there would be enough money for her dowry when she did find a man she could imagine marrying.

She had no aspirations to marry a titled gentleman, but it was rather nice to imagine that a man like Mr. Walsham might show interest in her this season. A handsome man, who made her feel fluttery, with eyes she could lose herself in…

Of course, she knew that most matches in this world did not take place because the lady found the gentleman attractive and kind. No, they were usually matters of business, arranged without much input from her at all, if any.

And she did not think she would mind too much if her brother sorted out the details—although she would have much preferred that her father was the one to do so. As long as the man was not unkind, and not so ancient that she would be a widow before she was twenty-five.

LAURENCE WAS SURPRISED to find that the pretty little redhead remained in his mind for the rest of the evening.

He did not know Carrington well; they'd been introduced at White's by a mutual acquaintance and had seen each other there on another couple of occasions. In truth, Laurence had not found the man particularly likable. But there was no reason to give him the cut direct, and so when he had called his name, he had, of course, been polite.

Had he asked the débutante to dance out of politeness? Not particularly. He liked to dance, especially with pretty young women—and there was something about her red hair that drew him in. Also, she had looked so lost, even among the sea of people. He had found himself wanting to draw her into the crowd instead of leaving her watching on with her brother.

He had definitely felt sorry for the shy redhead at Carrington's side, but he did not think that was the reason why he had asked her to dance. Nor was it the reason that she remained on his mind. He did not normally have any interest in débutantes, especially after he had danced with them once. He would never want to give a false impression or raise expectations. That was why his liaisons were limited to widows who understood the way things worked.

He struggled to picture himself married. He was sure it would happen one day, especially if he was to keep his word to his father, which he fully intended to do. But the idea of one woman expecting him to come home every night, expecting him to confide in her… presumably expecting him to be faithful…

He wasn't sure it was something he could do.

Perhaps he would have to find a wife who understood that those things could not be expected of him. That he was a free spirit, and that he did not wish to be contained. But neither would he wish to return home to a downcast wife who was hurt by his behavior.

As he enjoyed a whiskey in the card room, he hoped very much that the need to marry was many years in the future.

Hopefully, by then, a more settled life would appeal to him.

He watched the table where Oliver Carrington was playing and observed the man putting down more and more money, losing rather spectacularly to Baron Brett. Then he downed his drink and stormed out.

He certainly seemed rather a difficult fellow, and Laurence found himself hoping that his sister did not have to deal with the wrath he was surely feeling after such a loss at the card table.

"YOU SHOULDN'T DANCE with Mr. Walsham again," Oliver said as their coach rattled toward their home two hours later. It had been a long two hours, with Anastasia feeling awkward and alone, and now her brother was in a foul mood, having clearly lost a lot of money.

Anastasia frowned. "Why not? I thought he was a friend of yours and that he was to be a viscount someday."

"He is a perfectly good friend for me to have, and yes, one day he will be a viscount. But he will not marry the likes of you, and your reputation will be damaged if you spend much time with him."

She was glad it was dark enough that her brother was unlikely to see her wince at his harsh words. Of course, she didn't expect a viscount to ask for her, for she was an untitled lady with a modest dowry. But he didn't have to say it so cruelly.

"I doubt he will ever ask me to dance again, so I'm sure you need not worry. But pray tell, why on earth would my reputation be so damaged by another dance?"

"You must pay more attention to the gossip around you, Anastasia," Oliver said with a sigh. "The man is a renowned rake—a different woman every week, or so I'm told. The things that are said about him at White's…" He waved his hand in the air. "Well, they aren't really appropriate to share. Suffice it to say, he is not the sort of man you want people thinking you spend time with."

Anastasia felt her cheeks redden at even the mention of his rakish ways, without any of the salacious details. She had been fairly sheltered throughout her life and had no real knowledge of how the world worked; of what went on between men and women when they were not under society's close scrutiny. But she could not find herself all that surprised that a man like Mr. Walsham—handsome, charming, with that roguish smile—would be rather popular among the ladies of the ton.

And as her brother noted, she did not listen to gossip. She never had, and so she had not heard any whisperings about Mr. Walsham's character. She supposed her brother was only looking out for her, making sure she did not ruin her prospects so soon after they had re-entered society. Although she struggled to see what harm another dance could really do under the watchful eye of all those society matrons.

"I do not wish to be rude, especially to a future viscount," she said, trying to imagine a situation in which Mr. Walsham asked her to dance again and in which she said no. She could not fathom it.

"Well, as you say, it is unlikely to happen again. Perhaps I was foolish to introduce you. His partiality for redheads is well known. If it does happen, though, you will know to try to make some excuse—or else you are taking your reputation into your own hands."

# CHAPTER THREE

"YOU MUST NOT forget your vow to me," Viscount Walsham said in a raspy voice that only seemed to be growing weaker.

"Of course not, Father," Laurence said, although he was very much focused on the current predicament, not on how he would keep the vow he had made five years ago in Vauxhall Gardens.

While his father slept, Laurence sat in an armchair beside him and watched his fragile breathing. This problem with his heart had come on suddenly, and yet the situation had become dire so quickly. It was hard to believe the doctor's words—that his father had only days left to live—when only two weeks earlier, he had been the picture of health.

Laurence did not wish to imagine a world without him, so he refused. Instead, he let his mind wander to that vow he had made on a night five years earlier when his father had taken him to Vauxhall Gardens, and they had witnessed his uncle's foolhardy behavior.

IT HAD BEEN a dry, chilly night, and a rare one in which the viscount had decided he wished to go out in society. He was a quiet man, who liked to read and walk and spend time in gentle conversation—not a man who loved the loud thrills and excitements that London had to offer.

But that year, he had decided to accompany Laurence to London for the Season—perhaps to make sure he wasn't behaving as wildly as reports suggested. While they got on very well, Laurence and his father were like chalk and cheese. Laurence often wondered whether his mother had possessed a wild streak like he himself seemed to.

And so his father had joined him in London, although he had declined most invitations. However, having heard of the wonder of the Cascade at Vauxhall Gardens, he had decided to join his son—and it was just before the Cascade was turned on for the evening's performance that the viscount's younger brother, Laurence's uncle Thomas, had stumbled across their path, clearly extremely drunk and followed by two burly-looking men.

"Brother, dearest," he said, his eyes lighting up at the sight of them. "Gentlemen, I do not believe you have met my brother, Viscount Walsham."

By the looks on the two men's faces, they did not care at all to meet a viscount, and only one of them bowed his head in greeting.

"Give us our money, and we will be on our way—then you can spend all the time with your brother you wish," the shorter of the two men said.

Thomas visibly gulped.

"Well, you see, I don't quite have..." Thomas trailed off, his eyes darting left and right. If he thought his awkwardness would make the two men leave him alone, he was certainly mistaken.

"Perhaps your brother could lend you what you owe, so that everyone continues to have a... pleasant evening."

Laurence glanced at his father, who had remained silent throughout this exchange, and saw a nerve in his cheek twitch. Viscount Walsham was generally a calm and amiable man—but this was not always the case when he was around his brother.

"What does my brother owe?" the Viscount asked through gritted teeth.

"Two thousand pounds."

Thomas blanched, and Laurence's eyes widened. That was a lot of money to ask his father for offhand… it was also a lot of money to have lost, presumably in some sort of high-stakes game.

Although he clearly did not wish to, Laurence watched his father pull out a sheaf of notes and hand them to one of the men. "That's two hundred. If you visit my man of business tomorrow, he will give you the rest."

The man grinned toothily as Viscount Walsham relayed the address and then promptly disappeared into the crowd with his accomplice.

"Dominic, I can't thank you enough," Thomas said as soon as the two men had left. "It was just a bit of a misunderstanding, really. A bet which they took far more seriously than they ought to have done. I will pay you back, of course…"

Laurence's father shook his head. "When have you ever paid me back, Thomas? And how many times have you come to me with gambling debts or accounts owing? You had a generous inheritance from our father, and you could have made a good living in the army or as a clergyman. But you have frittered away every penny—"

Thomas narrowed his bloodshot eyes. "You have no idea what it is like to be a second son. To have none of the privilege—"

The viscount exhaled noisily. "You had every privilege growing up, Thomas. And you have more privilege now than most. You must take responsibility for your actions—for I will not always be here to do so."

Thomas opened his mouth to argue and then clearly thought better of it. "Well, I will bid you a good evening, brother, nephew."

It was then, when he had disappeared into the night, that Viscount Walsham had turned to his son and extracted the promise from him.

"The viscountcy cannot go to him," he said through gritted teeth, his face flushing red. "He would destroy it. Everything I have worked for, everything that generations of Walshams have worked for, would be gone in an instant if that man had control."

"You needn't worry, Father," Laurence said, realizing that they had missed the Cascade—the event they had come here to see. "The viscountcy will pass to me, and I will ensure it is not destroyed. I promise you."

His father shook his head. "I need you to promise more than that. You enjoy carousing and women a little too much, but I know you are a good man. I am not worried about the title or the estates under your care. You must promise me, here and now, that you will do your duty. That you will marry and produce an heir—several, ideally—to be certain that my brother will never get his hands on the title, the money, or the estates."

"Of course, Father," Laurence said, not really thinking about the words, keen to return his normally placid father to his usual nature.

"You must promise," his father said, reaching out and gripping his hand tightly. "You need not marry now—I know you are young and enjoying your freedom. But I only have the one son, and I have no intention of marrying again. So you must do this for me—and ensure that the title is passed down our line."

"I promise, Father." It did not seem like a particularly weighty vow to make. After all, he assumed he would marry one day and sire children. Of course, there was no way to guarantee he would have a boy… he would just have to trust in God for that. The idea of marriage at that time was not particularly appealing; his father was right—he did enjoy his freedom, and he had rather a growing reputation among the ladies of the ton. By the time it was necessary to think about marriage and producing an heir—and he hoped that was a very long time in the future—he would surely feel more ready for it.

"Do not leave it too long to marry," his father said that evening in his sick bed, after managing only a couple of mouthfuls of the soup that Cook had sent up to his bedroom for dinner. "You cannot know what the future holds. I wish you a long and happy life, my son—but you need to make sure you are married and have a son in case life is not that kind."

Laurence nodded, his eyes full of unshed tears. The world did not seem a kind place right now. He knew of many men who did not get on with their fathers, who would have been rather jubilant at the thought of inheriting the title, of finally becoming the person they had known they would be their whole lives.

But not Laurence. He was happy enough with the abstract idea of being a viscount. It did not hold any great terror for him. However, the thought of losing his beloved father was far too high a price to pay. He would have quite happily remained Mr. Walsham for the rest of his days if it meant keeping the man who had been a constant in his life by his side.

Of course, that was not his—nor his father's—decision to make.

"I will not break my vow, Father," Laurence said, taking hold of the man's thin, bony hand. "You do not need to worry on that score."

And he hoped that such knowledge eased his father's passing when he left the world later that night.

# CHAPTER FOUR

THE PROMISE WEIGHED on Laurence's mind in the months that followed. Grief overwhelmed him, and for a while, he retreated to the countryside. Not that he was sure being there helped. There were no distractions like there were in London, just endless memories of his beloved father.

And yet, he could not bring himself to return to London, to the life he had led before. It wasn't because he was now a viscount, or even out of a sense of duty—it was knowing that in London, he would be expected to be the old Laurence: fun and flirtatious, the life and soul of the party.

And at that moment in time, he simply did not have it in him to be so.

ANASTASIA WAS FINDING the Season even less enjoyable than she had anticipated. It wasn't just that her brother generally abandoned her in order to gamble and drink, although that was irritating enough. No, it was also the fact that the further they got into the Season, the more he insisted that she needed to marry for the good of the family.

He wanted her to find someone titled and wealthy, but she was not really sure what she had to offer. She thought she was fairly attractive, though she knew she often went unnoticed. And then there was the fact that, according to the rumors, her brother had frittered away the dowry that had been set aside for her by their father.

So she was shy, with no title and no money. Hardly an incredible prospect.

She had asked Oliver about her dowry when she had first heard the rumors, but his spiky reaction had stopped her from asking again.

She watched from the edge of another dance floor as couples moved in time with the music, laughed, drank, and flirted.

It was unlikely that her dance card would remain entirely empty; neither would she be overwhelmed by suitors eager to dance with her and call on her the following day with flowers.

And as time ticked on, Oliver grew more and more impatient.

"May I have this dance, Miss Carrington?"

Realizing she had been daydreaming, Anastasia forced her attention back to the present—where Baron Brett stood before her, grinning broadly with his hand outstretched.

A chill went down her spine. She had met the baron once or twice when he had come to their home to play cards with her brother, and again at several social functions. And it wasn't that he had done anything wrong, but there was just something about him that made her feel uneasy. The way his eyes seemed to rake down her body every time he saw her. The way he never seemed to pay attention to anything she was saying, even if he had been the one to select the topic of conversation.

The way he so often sought her out, whether her brother was there or not.

She hoped he was not getting any ideas of courting her, for he was surely older than her father would have been had he still been alive. The same age, at least. And although she knew Oliver wanted her married, she did not think she needed to settle for a man like Baron Brett. Oh, he had money and a title—but she did not believe there was any way he could make her happy. And the thought of kissing him, of allowing him to touch her...well, it sent another uncomfortable chill down her spine.

"That would be lovely, thank you," she replied, even though she really wanted to say no. Of course, to do so would be unconscionably rude. It would certainly anger her brother. And she always tried not to anger Oliver. It wasn't easy to calm him down, once he was riled.

He took her hand and led her to the dance floor, which was already filling up with couples ready for the next set.

"Is that a new gown?" the baron asked, his eyes resting for far too long on the neckline of her dress.

Anastasia felt a strong urge to cover up, but the music began, and there was no way she could use her fan to hide her décolletage from his incessant staring.

"It is," she simply replied.

"Well, you must allow me to say how becoming it is," he said when the music brought them together.

"Thank you."

In truth, she did not particularly like the new gown. It had been made before her father had died, when there had been money for such extravagances. But then he had passed, and the shade had been too bright to wear even in half-mourning. And so the dress had lain forgotten, untouched in the parcel it had been delivered in from the modiste.

Until Oliver had told her she needed to make more of an effort to attract a husband and had pulled it out, insisting it be worn. She supposed she had liked it when she had chosen it, but now the fabric seemed too bright, the neckline too daring, and the purpose of the dress left her melancholic.

She did not want to be trussed up to attract a husband. She would much rather do so with conversation, wit, and intelligence.

Of course, that was not the way these things worked. First, one attracted a gentleman with dresses like these and flirtatious smiles from behind a fan.

And then, if you were lucky, you got to know one another and discovered some compatibility.

She very much doubted that could ever be the case with Baron Brett. She thought he was attracted to her—but she was very much not attracted to him. And as to whether they had anything in common…his main interests seemed to be gambling and drinking. He would be far happier spending an evening conversing with Oliver than he would be with her, that was for certain.

# CHAPTER FIVE

"WE ARE TO go to Vauxhall Gardens tomorrow night," Oliver said as they broke their fast together one morning at the end of the Season.

Anastasia smiled. Of all the outings the Season offered, Vauxhall Gardens was one she actually enjoyed. Oh, there was still the same pressure to look for a husband—to try to be seen without being too obvious, to attract the attention of the right people. But there was also so much else to enjoy: the fireworks, the lamps, the Cascade. Performers and musicians, all with the sole purpose of entertaining and making the evening livelier.

They had not been in a long time, and Anastasia rather hoped it was a sign that her brother's mood was improving—that perhaps he would stop being so beastly to her and they could begin again as friends.

For since Father had died, he had seemed to view her only as a burden, never taking into account her feelings or thoughts. She was simply a problem that needed to be married off—and every day she wasn't wed only irritated him more.

But he knew she enjoyed the gardens, though she did not think he felt the same. After all, there was no card room at Vauxhall Gardens, although she was sure gentlemen managed to set up a game here and there. If a man wanted to gamble, he always found a way.

"Thank you, brother," she said as soon as she had finished a slice of toast. "I shall look forward to that."

He nodded. "Make sure you wear something nice—something that has not been seen before."

In truth, Anastasia did not believe there was a single item in her wardrobe that had not yet been seen out in society. She had not asked Oliver for more money for dresses since her period of mourning, when she had needed new clothes, and he had rather angrily told her that the funds were not there for her to fritter away.

But she did not wish to quarrel with him now—not when he seemed to be offering some sort of olive branch—and so she nodded and kept quiet. She would speak with her maid, and together she was sure they could rework one of her dresses so that it was not obviously one she had worn before. She doubted her brother paid that much attention to her fashion choices, in any case.

LAURENCE FELT RATHER flat being back in London. In the six months since his father had passed, he had seen very little of society, keeping to himself at his Kent estate and not responding to invitations to events in London or to house parties planned for after the Season had finished.

He had come to a point where solitude no longer seemed to help. He knew he could not spend the rest of his life in such a state—not only because it was not much of a life at all, rotting away in the countryside in his melancholy, but also because he needed to fulfill his promise to his father. He needed to find a wife and sire an heir.

On the carriage ride back to London, he had wondered how he might go about choosing a wife. He knew he had a rakish reputation among the ladies of the ton, and that the matchmaking mamas never wished for him to be around their precious daughters.

Surely that would change, though, if they knew he was actively seeking a wife? A title and a large fortune could forgive many sins, and he was sure that the matchmaking mamas of the ton simply wished for a good, respectable match for their daughters. Once he offered that layer of respectability, he thought his task might not be so difficult.

No, what would be harder would be finding a woman with whom he would wish to spend his life. He wasn't expecting some great love, necessarily. It wasn't that he didn't believe in it... He had seen his mother and father and knew that love for her was what had stopped his father from ever remarrying, ever having a second son in case anything happened to the first.

But he did not believe love was particularly common. He did not need to hold out for some great romance. And he supposed he did not even need to have anything in common with the woman he married. Once they had done their duty to the title, there was no reason they needed to even reside together, if they did not wish it. As Viscount Walsham, he owned multiple homes. There was nothing stopping him from setting her up in one and continuing his life as it had been before. Many men had mistresses.

And yet the thought of it made him feel uncomfortable. He had enjoyed his life before his father had died and had felt absolutely no guilt in the way he had spent his time. After all, no one had been hurt by his actions. The women had never expected anything more.

But a wife... A wife might well expect more. And he did not want to live with guilt or feel that he was letting her down.

And so, he rather thought, this stage of his life might be very, very different from what had come before it.

THE LAMPS WERE lit not long after Oliver and Anastasia arrived at Vauxhall Gardens. Anastasia could not help but smile at the sight of them. They brought a certain magic to the air, as if anything were possible.

"It is busy tonight," she commented as they made their way through the crowd to get some refreshment.

"People are getting ready to leave London for the end of the Season," Oliver said, taking two glasses of champagne and handing one to her. "They want one last night before they disappear back into the obscurity of the country."

"Will we quit London this year?" Anastasia asked, feeling for the first time in a long while that she could ask her brother a question without having her head snapped off.

The previous year, after Papa had passed away, they had gone to the country. Anastasia had thought it a sensible decision, for she had wished to mourn in peace and in private, and therefore staying in London had been rather pointless.

Before that year, her brother had tended to stay in London when most of the ton left for the countryside. He always seemed to have some group of friends who had no real wish to rusticate in the country, and, by his own admission, he was very bored when out of Town.

But he was the head of the family now, and he would make such decisions. She had no idea whether he would wish to follow precedent, leaving at the end of the month like the rest of society, or whether he would continue on his own path and keep them both in London even after everyone else had left.

He could still gamble and drink and see his friends, she supposed... But she rather thought the opportunities for her in London out of the Season would be limited. There would be no balls, no invitations to tea. Vauxhall Gardens would be closed, and there was only so much she wished to shop—especially considering they did not seem to have any money for such frivolity.

Oliver swapped his glass of champagne from one hand to the

other, then back again, before answering her question. "I am…thinking I will return to the country," he said slowly, not meeting her eye.

She smiled anyway. "That seems like an excellent plan. I will look forward to seeing the estate again. I enjoy London, but it always feels so wonderful to return home."

Oliver seemed to drink nearly half his glass of champagne in one gulp before gesturing to the opposite side of the gardens. "Ah, look, there's Baron Brett."

Anastasia groaned inwardly. That man always seemed to turn up wherever she was. And no matter how politely she tried to make it clear that she had no interest in any further dances with him, he was insistent.

"We should go over and greet him," Oliver said, finishing the rest of his champagne while Anastasia had only taken a sip of hers. The bubbles seemed to go right to her head as she said, "Must we? He'll only ask me to dance…"

"Yes, we must," Oliver said sharply, taking her elbow and roughly steering her in the baron's direction, her champagne sloshing in its glass as he did so.

"And you will be polite, and dance with him, and smile at his jokes, and generally charm him," Oliver ordered through gritted teeth.

"If that is what you wish, brother," Anastasia said with a sigh.

"It is," Oliver said, stopping abruptly not far from the baron. "And one other thing—he will wish to discuss your wedding this evening."

Anastasia frowned. "My wedding? Why on earth would Baron Brett wish to discuss an event that is not even planned to take place?"

Oliver's eyes darted away as he answered her. "Because it *is* planned to take place. You and Baron Brett will marry as soon as the banns can be read."

# CHAPTER SIX

Laurence did not know why he had decided to come to Vauxhall Gardens. Perhaps it was because he knew that the friends he might see at the club or even at a ball would be less likely to be at Vauxhall, especially this late in the Season.

Perhaps he was avoiding them, secluding himself even among the hubbub of the London season.

Or perhaps it was simply that the promise to his father weighed upon his mind, and since this was the place where it had happened, he somehow felt closer to his father by being here.

Whatever the reason, he knew he needed a drink, and so he stalked through the crowds to the refreshment table. In the middle of the melee, he spotted Oliver Carrington, wearing a pained expression, and that pretty redheaded sister of his looking unusually pale. He changed direction slightly, so that he might avoid them. The last thing he was in the mood for was pleasant chitchat, especially with a man like Carrington, whom he did not even like.

As he sipped a glass of champagne and watched the gardens come to life, he remembered what Miss Carrington had said to him about the loss of her father and the grief she had been feeling, earlier in the Season.

He had felt sorry for her at the time and had tried to imagine how she must have felt, but he had been unable to truly empathize.

Well, now he certainly understood… And how he wished he didn't.

Would he carry the pain of this loss forever? Would it ease as time passed? They always said that time healed all wounds, but he struggled to see how he could ever look on life the same way without the man who had taught him everything he knew—who had always been in the background, ready with advice whenever it was wanted.

"What are you talking about?" Anastasia asked, stopping abruptly. The baron was still making his way toward them, and horror filled every pore of her body. This had to be a joke—some elaborate jest on her brother's part. There was surely no way he could think…

"You are to marry Baron Brett," Oliver said, and Anastasia could hear her heart pounding in her ears. "You will have a position, a title, money—don't make a fuss about it."

"I cannot," Anastasia said. "I will not!" Her voice grew higher with every word, and she knew others around them could hear. The baron himself would soon be able to hear, but she could not control her anguish. "Oliver, you cannot be—"

"It is all arranged," Oliver said through gritted teeth. "I told you that you needed a husband, and now I have found you one. You should be grateful."

"He is old enough to be my father! And we have nothing in common! And the way he looks at me—"

"The man is attracted to you. You should take it as a compliment. That is a positive thing in a husband-to-be."

"He will not be my husband," Anastasia said, and as the baron reached them, she turned on her heel and ran.

Laurence was vaguely aware of some commotion in the center of the gardens, but he was more focused on trying to evade Lady Frindley, a widow with whom he'd had a liaison in the weeks before his father had died.

He had sent her word that he was leaving the city but had ignored any correspondence afterward, not wanting her to see it as an invitation to visit when he had no wish to socialize.

She had eyed him across the gardens and had immediately made a beeline for him, so he was trying to find somewhere he would not be found.

The point of his liaisons had always been that there were no expectations upon him. And while the lady certainly didn't expect marriage, he rather thought she would anticipate that they would pick up where they had left off six months earlier.

But things had changed. He was no longer the carefree, responsibility-free Mr. Walsham he had been before. Now he was the viscount, with his father's words ringing in his ears and a duty to marry and produce heirs to the title.

Would the widow appreciate that? Quite possibly. But it was not a conversation he wanted to have with her here, in the middle of a social event—his first such event since the death of his father.

And so he slunk away into the shadows, finding himself on the dark walk, where the lack of illumination gave him the opportunity to hide. He had hidden there before, although always accompanied—but tonight, he slipped through unnoticed by amorous couples, wondering if coming out in society had been a mistake.

Tears blurred Anastasia's vision as she moved through the crowd, aware that she was probably causing gossip but unable to care. How could Oliver possibly think she would happily marry

Baron Brett? Had she not made her distaste for him apparent? Let alone the fact that they were so far apart in age?

And he had not even asked her… He had simply given the order and expected it to be obeyed.

She really was just a burden—something to be disposed of.

She was pleased when the crowd thinned, and she felt the eyes of scrutiny no longer upon her. The illuminations faded, and she found herself among trees and shrubs, with no light save for the moon to guide her. She stumbled, tears falling down her cheeks, and landed against something soft and warm.

"Watch where you're going!" a voice said, and in horror, Anastasia realized she had stumbled across a couple in an amorous embrace.

She jumped away and ran further into this side of Vauxhall Gardens, which she had never seen before, rather shocked to find that there was more than one couple hidden away here, enjoying each other's company in ways that certainly would not be permitted if society knew. Or if society saw…which, she supposed, was the point of this dark, secluded place.

Had she been in her right mind, she might have considered that even being down this dark walk could be enough to ruin her reputation, but all she could think about was getting away from her brother and Baron Brett and trying to figure out what on earth she was meant to do now.

She did not think her brother could force her to marry him…but he could certainly make her life very difficult if she refused. Would he throw her out onto the streets? Before, she would not have thought so. He'd had his cruel moments, over the years, but she'd always believed he cared for her enough not to see her homeless. She also would not have thought that he would have arranged for her to marry a man without even asking her.

She was beginning to think that she did not know her brother at all.

She found a stone bench, mercifully unoccupied, and took a

seat, shivering in her thin gown.

As soon as she sat down on the cold stone, tears poured down her face, and she hiccupped, unable to regain control.

Her life was over, ruined...and she had absolutely no idea what to do about it.

# CHAPTER SEVEN

THE SOUND OF sobbing caught Laurence's attention, for it was very different from the giggles, amorous sounds, and hushed whispers that filled the dark walk.

He walked toward the sound, unable to help himself—wanting to be of assistance if someone was hurt.

The only light came from the moon, which, thankfully, had appeared from behind the clouds, and as he entered the clearing, he spotted the source of the sobbing.

It was a redheaded woman, her head in her hands, shoulders shaking as she cried.

He cleared his throat, not wanting to startle her, but she jumped anyway.

Even in the moonlight, he could see the anguish on her face, and he found he recognized her: she was Carrington's sister, the pretty young woman he had danced with months before. He was rather surprised that he remembered that. He danced with a lot of women, and they did not all remain firmly in his memory.

"Is all well?" he asked, even though it clearly was not.

She sniffed and shivered a little, and he immediately shrugged off his jacket and handed it to her. "The night is getting chilly—you don't want to fall ill."

She reached out and took the coat, slipping it around her shoulders. It nearly drowned her petite frame, but at least she would not be so cold.

"Can you tell me what's happened? It cannot be as bad as all this, surely…"

He was pleased to see that her clothes showed no sign of any struggle with some disreputable man, but he had no idea as to the cause of her anguish.

She gave him a sad smile. "No, I'm sure it cannot be that bad. I'll be all right in a minute, Mr.—Lord Walsham. Thank you."

So it seemed she remembered him too—and also knew of his change in status, and therefore, the death of his father.

He took a seat beside her on the stone bench, wincing as the cold of the stone chilled his skin even through his coat. "This isn't a good place to be hiding, you know."

From so close, he saw her cheeks flushed red and wondered what she had seen that had sent her running through the dark walk to this sanctuary.

"I just had to get away from… from them. Just while I figured out what to do…"

Laurence frowned. "Get away from whom? And what is it you need to sort out?"

Anastasia was very grateful for the viscount's jacket, but she did not wish to explain herself to anyone. She could not talk about Baron Brett and the proposed marriage between them without feeling as though she might be sick—and she certainly did not wish for that to happen in front of this handsome viscount whom she had danced with once, many months earlier.

She knew she shouldn't be here, let alone alone with a gentleman—but with her only other option being to return to the main gardens and face her brother, she thought possible ruin seemed less terrifying.

"I can escort you back to the dance floor, if you wish. Your brother must be—"

At the mention of Oliver, she could not control herself and let out a sob.

"Has your brother done something, Miss Carrington?" he

asked, and Anastasia did not know what to say.

"Perhaps I could speak with him on your behalf, if you would just tell me—"

Anastasia shook her head. "I don't think he'd listen. Not to me, not to you… His head is so filled with thoughts of debts and gambling and the life he thinks he should be leading… I just don't see—" Her voice cracked.

It was ever so hard to admit the truth: that she could not see any way out of marrying the baron unless she intended to become a penniless outcast. She did not know if she could survive that. She had no other family to rely on…only Oliver. And he clearly did not care.

The tears began to flow down her cheeks once more, and she buried her head in her hands, hoping that the viscount would find the situation awkward and leave rather than press her for more details. He seemed a very pleasant man, although apparently he had a wicked reputation, but she could not confide in him. She could not confide in anyone.

She was surprised by the feeling of a strong arm around her shoulders, and when she looked up, she found the viscount was looking down at her with pity in his eyes. The warmth from his body seeped through the jacket, and she leaned into it, despite knowing it was wrong. She could not remember the last time anyone had comforted her, the last time anyone had held her…

She took a deep, shuddering breath, and just for a moment, lay her head against his shoulder and soaked up the feeling that somebody cared about her.

"My, my, what do we have here?" a matronly voice called out, and Anastasia jumped away from the viscount, his jacket falling from her shoulders as she did so.

But it was too late.

Standing in a gap in the shrubbery was the imposing figure of the Duchess of Tewkesbury, with three ladies behind her, gasping behind their fans.

"I—this—it—" No sensible words would come out of her

mouth. "Your Grace," she managed to say in a pleading voice. "I—"

"You are alone in the arms of a gentleman in the dark walk, Miss Carrington. My, when your brother said he could not find you, I never expected…"

# CHAPTER EIGHT

DESPITE HIS NOTORIOUSLY rakish ways, Laurence had never before found himself in a position like this. And what was more ridiculous was that, unlike with other dalliances, nothing had happened. He had merely tried to comfort the distraught girl—but clearly that had been a mistake.

He should have known to leave well enough alone. Perhaps the grief had softened his heart, for he was no fool; he didn't need to be told how being discovered with his arm around an eligible young lady in a dark corner would look. And discovered by the Duchess of Tewkesbury, no less—who was as well known for gossiping as Laurence was for womanizing.

"I can assure you, Your Grace," Laurence began, standing up to address the old lady, "you are mistaken. Miss Carrington was upset, and I was just offering to escort her back to her brother."

The duchess tutted. "A likely story. Do not think I am unaware of your reputation, Lord Walsham."

Laurence gritted his teeth and tried very hard not to look as irritated as he felt. He had tried to be kind, but instead was being accused of inappropriate behavior. It did not really seem fair. And he hadn't so much as kissed the young woman. Perhaps, for a moment, he had considered it...but then his sensibility had returned, and he had not followed through with such a desire.

Miss Carrington stood. She had managed to stop crying, and she faced the duchess with a surprising amount of bravery.

"Your Grace," she said, finally seeming to find her tongue, "Lord Walsham's words are true. I was upset because of something my brother said, and I foolishly ran in here. He was merely making sure I was not hurt."

The duchess narrowed her eyes. "And what exactly were *you* doing on the dark walk, Lord Walsham, if not pursuing a conquest?"

Laurence sighed and fought the desire to roll his eyes. "If you must know," he said, eying the ladies behind the duchess and wondering if his words would shock them, "I was avoiding a lady with whom I have an…acquaintance. One I did not wish to see."

The duchess laughed. "Oh yes, the dark walk is well known as a place to hide from amorous encounters, rather than seek them out," she said with a hearty dose of sarcasm. "I'm afraid we find ourselves in a bit of a situation here. As you must be aware, Lord Walsham, your presence with this girl—with your arm around her, your clothes upon her—has utterly ruined her reputation."

Laurence closed his eyes momentarily as Miss Carrington gasped beside him. This entire thing was ridiculous: the idea that he had ruined the girl simply by checking whether she was all right. Very well, it was not the best location for such activity, but that did not mean…

"What is the meaning of this?" a male voice said, joining the group in the clearing. Laurence rather expected it to be Carrington, but although he was there too, it was not his voice that had spoken.

"Baron Brett. Mr. Carrington. I'm afraid we have a situation here," the Duchess of Tewkesbury said, clearly delighting in being involved in such drama. Did she not care that she was ruining this girl's reputation, her chances at a decent marriage? Or was she entirely intent on ensuring that this encounter ended in a very good marriage indeed…

Even though he knew he needed to find a wife, the thought still sent a shiver down his spine. He had spent a long time avoiding getting shackled, and he had not thought that he would somehow find himself trapped into being so, with very little say in the matter or choice in the bride.

"I can see that," Baron Brett said, anger filling his face. Laurence wondered who he was and what connection he had to the Carringtons. Perhaps he was some uncle? He certainly looked of an age to be.

"Oliver, I can promise—" Miss Carrington began.

"Be quiet, you silly girl," Mr. Carrington said, and Laurence found his dislike for the man growing. "What have you done? You've ruined everything, and why? To spite me?"

Miss Carrington shook her head furiously. "No, I have not, I promise—"

"I see no other option," the duchess said, a small smile playing upon her lips. "She is ruined. You will have to marry her, Walsham. And quickly."

"No!"

The protest did not come from Miss Carrington, as he might have expected, or from her brother—but from Baron Brett, whose face was clearly red, even in moonlight.

"This is not to be borne, Carrington. We had an agreement—you cannot just…"

"You can still marry her," Mr. Carrington said, and it became apparent to Laurence why Miss Carrington had run away, why she had been so upset.

"Things don't have to change. We'll hurry things along. I can pay for a special license—"

Baron Brett sneered. "With what money? And besides, she is not worth the same now. She is ruined, as the duchess said. Why on earth would I pay the same for spoiled goods as I would have done for a chaste bride?"

Laurence turned to look at Miss Carrington—partly to see her reaction and partly to stop himself from punching the obnoxious baron. It seemed that she had not known the full extent of the situation, for her features were frozen in a look of horror, and then her eyes darted between her brother and the man who was clearly expecting to marry her as a form of payment.

Carrington cleared his throat. "The girl must marry, yes, but there is no need for anyone to know of—"

And he could not say exactly why he did it, but Laurence found himself saying, "I have ruined her. I will marry her."

# CHAPTER NINE

ANASTASIA STUMBLED BACK in shock until her knees hit the stone bench, and she sat down forcefully. She could not believe what she was hearing. It had been bad enough knowing that her brother had arranged a match between her and Baron Brett without even caring what she thought. And then to be discovered with Lord Walsham, and it be assumed that something had happened…

But this…this was something else. Her brother seemed to be, in essence, selling her to the baron…or that had been his plan.

And now the viscount was saying he would marry her. It was hard to fully comprehend the words coming out of his mouth.

"Oh, you *will* marry her," the duchess said, looking very pleased with herself. "I am pleased to hear it. It is the right thing to be done."

"Miss Carrington was already betrothed," Oliver said desperately, and in the recesses of her panicked mind, Anastasia found herself wondering why the betrothal was so essential to him.

"I have seen nothing official," the duchess said coldly. "Miss Carrington, were you betrothed to this man?"

Anastasia shook her head. It seemed that one way or another she would end up betrothed by the end of this evening—and she could not marry Baron Brett. It was not just his age, but something about him that made her ever so uneasy.

"Well, there we go then. No one is ruined, and we shall have a wedding to end the Season." She clapped her hands together. "I think this has all turned out rather marvelously, if I do say so myself. Come now, ladies. And you, Lord Brett. Let us leave the Carringtons and Lord Walsham."

Anastasia picked up the viscount's jacket from where it had fallen on the ground but it did not seem capable of stopping her shivering, as the duchess, her companions, and the vile Baron Brett left the clearing.

And so she was left alone with the two men who, it seemed, would change her life forever—her brother, who had seemingly been willing to sell her to a man she despised, and Lord Walsham, whom she barely knew and would apparently be marrying.

She didn't have it in her to feel sorry for him, for the fact that he had been maneuvered into this marriage just as much as she had. For, of course, she knew that he had only been trying to comfort her, that nothing truly inappropriate had happened—but if they didn't believe him, they certainly weren't going to believe her.

Her thoughts were consumed with the enormity of what had just happened, and with the revelation of her brother's betrayal. Oliver and Lord Walsham were facing each other, and she realized then how small her brother looked, how insecure, compared to the imposing figure of Lord Walsham. For some reason, that realization satisfied her immensely.

"You have ruined my—" Oliver began, before the viscount smoothly interrupted.

"I can assure you I have not ruined your sister. But I understand that by being seen here with me today, her reputation has been compromised, and so I will marry her. You do not need to worry on that score."

Oliver gave her a scathing look, and then turned back to the viscount. "She has no dowry."

WAS THE MAN trying to give reasons for Laurence to back out? It seemed an odd thing to do in the situation. Laurence did not care that she did not have a dowry. He was not in need of any more money. He was in need of a wife—and this one had rather been dropped into his lap.

He had planned to make his selection with a little more thought, but the truth was that he had intended to marry this Season in order to fulfill his promise to his father—and he was certainly not going to allow Miss Carrington's reputation to be destroyed while he went off to find another wife.

No, that was not the man he was. And since he had not intended to marry for love anyway, it did not seem to matter too much that he had not planned to become betrothed to Miss Carrington. She seemed pleasant, and she was certainly attractive—what more did he need?

THE CARRIAGE JOURNEY home was not a comfortable one. Oliver simply glared at her, stared out of the window, and wrung his hands. Anastasia felt in turns too angry, and too shocked, to say anything to him. How could her own brother be willing to sell her—and to a man like Baron Brett?

And how was she now betrothed to Lord Walsham?

"You've ruined everything," Oliver said once the butler had closed the front door. He didn't even wait for them to be alone. He had obviously been stewing over this for the entire carriage ride.

Anastasia didn't know whether to scream or cry. How dare he accuse her of ruining everything after what *he* had done?

"You were going to make me marry that man. He is old enough to be my father—my grandfather! He doesn't want me; he just wants a young, biddable wife. Why, Oliver? Why would you do that to me? *How* could you do that to me?"

He had the grace to at least look a little embarrassed, his eyes shifting away from hers, his fingers squirming into fists as if he did not know what to do with them.

"And how am I to pay him now?" he asked, pacing the corridor. The butler had disappeared, clearly sensing that this was not a conversation he ought to be overhearing. Anastasia was still wearing her cloak, and they had not even made it past the drafty hallway.

Anastasia frowned. "Pay him what? I don't understand, Oliver."

"I owe Baron Brett money. A great deal of money, if truth be told. And now…"

The blood ran cold in Anastasia's veins. When she had thought he was selling her off to the highest bidder, she had not literally thought that she was the payment for a debt. And apparently, she was. Nothing more than a promissory note, or a pile of gold coins, shoved across a table in order to fulfill a gambling debt.

"But he was willing to take me in payment," she said coldly. "Oh, Oliver. How could you?"

"You have no idea how hard it is to be the head of the family, to make sure the accounts balance, to look after you, to pay the staff. No idea at all. So don't you dare ask me how I could. I arranged a perfectly respectable marriage for you—and you ruined it, with your light-skirted ways. I never thought you could act so immorally, but I guess I was wrong."

"How can you lecture me on immorality when you were willing to use your own sister in payment of a debt—a debt you accrued through gambling away your inheritance?" Anastasia shouted back, no longer able to keep a lid on her emotions. She did not feel the need to correct his assumptions about her liaison with Lord Walsham. What was the point? They were to be wed anyway—and if she had to marry now, without the benefit of a love match, then Lord Walsham was certainly a far more attractive prospect than Baron Brett.

"Hold your tongue," Oliver said, his eyes narrowing as he took a step toward her. "You are a woman, and therefore you know nothing of my affairs, or the position of responsibility I am in. You have ruined a perfectly good plan. All we can be grateful for is that Lord Walsham was willing to do the right thing. Without me needing to call him out."

If such a situation had occurred, Anastasia could not imagine her scrawny brother standing a chance against the tall, statuesque Lord Walsham—but she certainly didn't voice this thought.

"Yes," Oliver continued, seemingly more to himself than to her. "You will be a viscountess soon. Well, that certainly brings power and money." He looked her dead in the eye. "You can fix this mess that you created once you've married him. Your new husband certainly has enough money to not miss some."

LAURENCE HEADED STRAIGHT for his study when he returned home and poured himself a large glass of brandy before taking a seat behind the oak desk.

This room always made him think of his father. It was his father whom Laurence pictured in the solid wooden chair which he now occupied.

But it was his chair now. His home. His title. And now he would fulfill his last promise to his father, by taking a wife—and, hopefully, siring multiple heirs.

He felt surprisingly calm about the prospect. It was not how he had intended for things to pan out, but it certainly wasn't the worst outcome. He simply needed to get things in order. He would need to procure a special license, in order to avoid any further damage to Miss Carrington's name. Why, in the three weeks it would take for the banns to be read, who knew what gossip the Duchess of Tewkesbury and her companions might spread? They were bored widows, and weaving intricate tales about the society they inhabited was their greatest form of joy.

Now that it had been decided that they were to marry, he thought they should do so as quickly as possible. He hoped Miss Carrington would be in agreement; he presumed she would, since it was her reputation he was concerned with defending. And besides, he rather thought she might be keen to get away from her brother—a man who had clearly been willing to marry her off for his own benefit, with no thought to her happiness.

He could be a better husband than Baron Brett, that was for certain. He had never planned to follow his heart into some wild love match; and while he might have picked a little more prudently, Miss Carrington was not an inappropriate choice to be his viscountess. Surely they could forge a happy life together, even if it was born of a scandal that had never really existed.

# CHAPTER TEN

As ELSIE—WHO WAS not a proper lady's maid, but more a maid of all work—dressed her on the morning of her wedding, Anastasia had never felt so alone.

She had barely spoken to her brother in the three days since the events at Vauxhall Gardens. She still couldn't believe he had intended to marry her off to Baron Brett. And she had no one else: no father to give her away, no mother to give her advice about the wedding, the wedding night, or marriage in general.

She was alone in the world and about to tie herself to a man she hardly knew at all. She didn't even know much about him. She knew he was handsome, that he was a good dancer, and that he had a reputation as a rake. Hardly much to build a marriage on.

"You look lovely, miss," Elsie said, a shy smile on her face. "And don't worry about your nerves, it's common to feel that way on your wedding day, or so I'm told."

Anastasia tried to smile back at her, but she wasn't sure if she was successful. The muscles in her mouth did not seem to want to do what she was willing them to. She certainly had not told the maid that she was nervous, but she had also barely spoken, so she supposed it was obvious.

And who wouldn't be nervous on their wedding day—let alone when one was marrying a man with whom one had only shared a handful of sentences?

She felt like she was watching herself from above as she put on the gloves that Elsie handed her and checked her appearance in the looking glass. It didn't feel like it was really her, but rather some girl in a play to which this was all happening. She knew her life was about to change immeasurably, and she could not quite fathom it.

Oliver was waiting in the carriage, dressed in his finest velvet waistcoat. His mood about the marriage seemed to have improved, in spite of the fact that Anastasia had barely spoken to him. More than once he had mentioned—without comment from Anastasia—how useful it would be to have a viscount for a brother-in-law.

Anastasia was finding it hard enough to accept that she would soon have a viscount for a husband. She could not also think about her brother's problems, or what he hoped to gain from this surprising marriage.

The church was small and rather nondescript. Anastasia had attended services there on Sundays when they were in town, occasionally accompanied by her brother, although far less often of late. She had never imagined marrying there, though. She had always thought that when she did wed, the marriage would take place in the beautiful church at the top of the hill in Cheltenham, where her family owned an estate. She had thought it would be an event planned over weeks or months, not days. There hadn't even been time for her to order a new gown; Elsie had merely made the best of one of her newest blue day dresses. Not that Anastasia could find it in herself to care all that much. She didn't even know who would be there to see it. Her new husband, of course, although it felt very odd to think of him in such terms, and Oliver—but she had no wish to impress him right now. She supposed there would have to be another witness, but she had no idea who it would be. Everything had been left to Lord Walsham—or *Laurence*, as she had discovered his Christian name to be. He had simply sent a note with the time and date of the ceremony, and his hopes that Miss Carrington was well. There had been no words of warmth towards Oliver, and Anastasia had seen the irritation cross her brother's face as he read the note.

She rather thought that her brother would not find a friend in Lord Walsham, his soon-to-be brother-in-law. He had not looked very impressed at the way things had been dealt with in Vauxhall Gardens—and although Oliver was her family, she was rather inclined to agree with him.

THERE WERE A handful of people in the church, but Laurence did not recognize any of them, save for Lord Stanley, whom he had asked to come along as a second witness, along with Miss Carrington's brother.

He supposed the others were just interested Londoners. He wasn't sure how they knew about the wedding, but he supposed when a viscount—and a notorious rake at that—suddenly ended up getting married, rumors spread. And while it was possible that no one respectable would particularly wish to attend this wedding, there were many who would be interested to see it, and say they had been in attendance.

He stood before the altar with Lord Stanley, feeling as though it were not really him standing at the front of the church, but instead someone who looked like him, sounded like him, felt like him—but an impostor.

A flash of red hair caught Laurence's eye, but it was not the vibrant red of his bride-to-be's, rather a paler, weaker shade. His eyes locked with the redhead's, and his pulse quickened, although he tried not to let it show.

*Lady Frindley.* What on earth was she doing there? The widow had, in rather a roundabout way, been responsible for him ending up in this very situation. Why, if he had not been trying to avoid her that night at Vauxhall Gardens, he surely would never have ended up on the dark walk—and never been seen comforting

Miss Carrington by the duchess.

It wasn't excitement that quickened his pulse, but irritation and concern. Was she here to make a scene? He had no idea what she hoped to gain, for he was sure that they had both always been clear on the fact that there was never any chance of them getting married.

But then, she had not accepted that things were over, so perhaps she wanted to stop him marrying… And that would not be fair to Miss Carrington. Anastasia. This might not be a love match, but she deserved more respect than that. Her brother had wanted to marry her off to an elderly, money-grabbing baron, and now she had been trapped in a marriage with him to save her reputation. He wanted to make her happy—and not destroy her reputation further. She was already marrying a well-known rake; she did not need the ignominy of having her husband's ex-lover making a scene at her wedding.

"Stanley," he muttered under his breath, aware that while the guests waited for Miss Carrington, their attention was on him.

His friend turned and raised an eyebrow. "Not wanting to make a run for it, are you?"

"No," Laurence said, and even he was surprised at the amount of conviction he felt. This marriage might not have happened in the way he had planned, but he had no intention of running away. He wouldn't ruin Miss Carrington like that, nor turn away from this marriage now. "But I need you to speak to someone for me. Quickly."

"I am at your service," Stanley said, with a mock bow. They had been friends for a long time, and usually Laurence found his joviality amusing. But today, he rather wished for some more gravitas.

"The redheaded lady, at the back of the church. Lady Frindley. I need to know that she will not make a scene."

Stanley raised an eyebrow. "And how exactly do you think I can achieve that, with your betrothed due at any moment?"

Laurence gritted his teeth. "Just find out why she is here. And if she has any intention to cause a scene, make it clear that nothing will change the outcome of today. Miss Carrington will be Lady Walsham by the end of the morning."

He shifted his weight uneasily as he watched his friend approach the widow. There was already an air of scandal about this wedding. That seemed to have kept the matchmaking Duchess of Tewkesbury away, at any rate. They didn't need Lady Frindley adding to the drama.

He watched as an irritated pout graced his former lover's face, and her back clearly stiffened. Stanley remained smiling, but Laurence thought his expression tightened, although it was hard to be sure from this distance.

For a moment, it looked as though they might have some sort of standoff, but then the church doors opened, and the vicar made it clear it was time for everyone to take their seats.

And thankfully, Lady Frindley complied.

As the organ music started up, Stanley returned to his side, and it was then that the nerves began to flutter in his stomach, as the full gravity of what he was about to do sank in.

He was going to marry this woman he barely knew. This was forever—a bond that could not be broken.

And in doing so, he would be fulfilling his final promise to his father. Well, fulfilling part of it, anyway. Then they needed to produce an heir to make sure that his father's brother never ended up as Viscount Walsham.

# CHAPTER ELEVEN

As SHE TOOK her first step into the church, Anastasia thought she might faint. Her brother walked beside her, giving her away because that was how things were done—not because she particularly wanted him to. After whom he had been willing to give her away to, she didn't really feel that he had the right.

It seemed rather strange how drastically things would change after she said a few words at that altar. She had always been her father's responsibility, and then her brother's—but once those words were said, she would no longer be a Carrington. She would belong to Lord Walsham—and she just hoped that her impression of him as a kind man, in spite of his reputation, was accurate.

She would be a viscountess. It was a higher rank than she had ever possibly thought to obtain. And she had no idea what to expect, nor how such a task was to be managed. Even if she had thought she might one day rank so highly, there was no one to teach her what was expected. Her mother was long dead, and had her beloved father had any knowledge of such things, he was also gone.

She didn't even know what was really expected of a wife. What her wedding night would entail...

She had heard the occasional wry, bawdy joke, but nobody had felt the need to explain the facts of life to her, and so she found herself entering into this sacred covenant even more naive than most young women.

She carried this fear of the unknown with her as she walked down the aisle to meet her fate. He was so tall—taller than she remembered, even though it had been mere days since the encounter on the dark walk. And even in her haze of fear and panic, she could acknowledge how devastatingly handsome he was. Handsome enough—and rich enough, as her brother had regularly reminded her—that his reputation could be overlooked by many.

Time seemed to slow down as she walked the short distance, and she was almost surprised when she found herself at the front of the church, with all eyes upon her and the viscount.

As Oliver passed her hand into his, she felt a jolt, a spark, fizzle through her at that point of contact, even through her white gloves.

"Please be seated," the vicar said, and so it began.

She said the words that she was asked to repeat, but had she been asked afterwards, she was not sure she could have remembered a single one of them. She did remember the moment he put a ring on her finger, and those binding words were said: "I now pronounce you man and wife."

She was a wife. A totally different person than she had been when she had walked into that church such a brief time earlier.

It did not feel entirely natural to have her arm threaded through Laurence's, but he was a strong, steady presence beside her, and he gave her a little more confidence as they walked through the surprisingly large crowd of guests who had gathered to witness their nuptials.

He didn't speak to her, though, until they were alone in the carriage, rattling off toward his London home, where they were to have a wedding breakfast.

"You look a little pale," he said, his brow furrowing in concern. "There were certainly more guests in attendance than I expected."

Her mouth felt unbearably dry, and it took her a moment to

be able to speak. "It is all rather overwhelming," she admitted in a small voice. "It... It has all happened so quickly. I feel like I cannot get my bearings."

She wasn't sure where the burst of honesty had come from. She had not really spoken about this wedding with anyone. She and Oliver were barely speaking, and when they were, it was not a topic she wished to discuss with him. She had also not felt as though it was something she wished to mention to her maid, even though they were friendly. She did not wish to start her tenure as a viscountess with gossip about how she had not felt prepared for such a task.

But, she reasoned, surely he understood how strange it felt to suddenly be making one of the biggest steps of one's life, without any knowledge that it was to happen so soon? He had also been dragged along for this dizzying ride, like a man who had fallen from his horse and had one foot caught in the stirrup as the horse bolted for freedom.

Neither of them had chosen this. Neither of them had expected it. But they would both have to make the best of things, if they were to live a happy life.

SHE LOOKED SMALL and scared, seated opposite him in the carriage, and he felt that same urge to take her into his arms and comfort her, as he had done in Vauxhall Gardens. Today, there was nothing stopping him from acting upon it, and yet, he found he could not. Look at where that embrace had led him. And besides, it felt different now. Like it meant something more...like it should be accompanied by some sort of grand statement, one he had not thought to make.

He hoped she was not feeling too pressured by the day. It had certainly been rather a surprising week, and he could see how the day could be overwhelming. But he did not wish for her to look so afraid, so pale, so alone. Because she wasn't alone. He had promised to be there for her in sickness and in health, until death they did part—and so she would never be alone again.

And neither would he.

"Our guests need not stay long," Lord Walsham said. "Of course, it is traditional that we have a wedding breakfast, and people will talk if we do not. But we have only invited a handful of people back to the house. And then…it will just be us."

# CHAPTER TWELVE

Anastasia nodded. She did not know what to say to this man who was now her husband. She was relieved that she would not have to socialize for too long, for her head felt rather muddled. And yet, she was somewhat fearful of the moment when everyone left—of what would be expected of her, of whether she would know how to assimilate into this new life of hers.

"Anastasia," he said, and the sound of her Christian name on his lips sent a jolt of awareness through her body, and her eyes snapped up to meet his.

"I know this marriage has not come about in the way either of us might have expected. But I want you to know that I mean to make you happy—or do my best, at least."

She tried to smile, because the words he was saying were kind, even if they could not allay all her fears. "I will do my best to be a good wife to you," she promised. "I do not know exactly what it means to be a wife, let alone a viscountess, but I mean to try."

He smiled back at her, and she was sure it was a much more confident smile than she had offered. Then he took her hands in his.

"We can learn together. Neither of us has been married before; neither of us knows exactly what we are going into."

And yet, Anastasia thought, he certainly knew a lot more

than she did. Perhaps he had not been married, but from the rumors that constantly swirled around him, he had known a good many women in the way one would know a wife.

She pushed that thought from her mind, for it only made her more nervous, and tried to look to her future with confidence.

"We will face it together then, Lord Walsham," she said, very aware that he was still holding her hands.

The corners of his mouth turned up even wider, and there was a twinkle in his eye. "I think perhaps you should call me *Laurence* now."

She nodded. "Of course. I'm sorry, I—"

"Nothing to apologize for. It's rather strange how everything can change, isn't it? Yesterday I was Lord Walsham; today I'm Laurence. Yesterday you were Miss Carrington, and today... well, you're Lady Walsham. Anastasia..." He smiled, as though the thought pleased him, and then carried on. "Besides, I still find myself thinking only of my father when I hear 'Lord Walsham.'"

Anastasia squeezed his hands. She certainly understood the pain of such a loss. And she had not thought before how it must be compounded for a man with a title—for he stepped into his father's shoes, taking even his name. If one had no relationship with one's father, she supposed it was merely a promotion to the higher ranks. But Lord Walsham—Laurence—had clearly loved his father.

"Of course. You must miss him..."

Laurence's jaw tightened. "Yes, every day."

She gave him a sad smile. "I can't quite say it gets easier, for I still think of my father nearly every day. Especially today..." She glanced out of the small carriage window to give herself a moment to compose herself, for the conversation had turned her misty-eyed. "But it does get easier to manage. The grief doesn't lessen, but you learn how to live with it."

HE HAD NOT spoken openly with anyone about his father's death, or how deeply the grief had taken hold. But Anastasia seemed to understand, to empathize, in a way he had not quite expected. And so it was easy to open up to her. He wished she had not felt the same pain that he had, and yet it brought them together, allowed them a moment of similarity in this very strange situation.

The coach ground to a halt, and the footman opened the door, allowing sunlight to stream in.

Laurence hopped out, leaving the heavy conversation in the carriage, and offered her his arm. "Allow me to escort you into your new home, Lady Walsham."

He felt a rather boyish excitement at entering his home with this pretty redhead on his arm, ebullient with the notion that he could give her a happier life than she would have otherwise known; excited to show her everything he had, everything he was more than willing to share with her.

There was something rather wonderful about no longer being alone. He had not realized how alone he'd felt until he suddenly wasn't. The women who had warmed his bed for most of his adult years had provided some company, some pleasure—but they were not women that he had ever planned to share his life with, to share his home with, or have children with. This was a new chapter, and he rather thought his father had set him on a path that was right for him.

He had never stayed with one woman more than a couple of months, finding his wish for change, the feeling of being stuck, always got too much around that time. But surely, with a wife, it would be different? Surely he would not feel like she was trying to trap him, when the marriage had been his suggestion. Perhaps it was still a trap, but it was a trap of his own making. And as she stepped into the parlor, looking even more petite in her nervousness, he hoped he would make her a good husband, and not give in to the temptations that had ruled his life thus far.

A SHIVER RAN through her body which had nothing to do with the chill in the air. The maid—Anastasia couldn't even remember her name—had helped her dress for bed without much conversation, and now she was alone. Waiting.

She knew from her earlier tour of the house that the viscount's room—Laurence's room—was on the other side of the oak door. And now that her maid had left her alone, *dressed in a nightgown that was the only familiar thing in this room, several seasons old, one purchased when Papa had been alive and everything had been different,* surely he would soon join her.

And she hadn't a clue what to expect.

She did not think she had ever felt as frightened as she did that night, waiting for Laurence, waiting for her wedding night, waiting for this unknown marital act that could produce children.

The clock on the mantelpiece ticked loudly and Anastasia tried to focus on the sound, tried to breathe in time with it, tried to slow her pulse and her racing thoughts.

But it was no use.

The soft knock on the interconnecting door made her jump, and it took a moment for her nerves to calm enough to allow her to call, "Come in."

She took a deep breath before turning to face him. His hair was damp, presumably from a recent bath, and he wore a dark blue dressing gown which stopped just below his knees. Her eyes roamed down the defined muscles of his calves and she gulped. It was more than she had ever seen of a man, outside of her brother when they were both children, and yet she was sure that before the night was out, she would see much more.

"Is the room to your liking?" he asked in his deep, steady voice.

She nodded, unsure whether she could speak without her voice shaking.

"And your belongings arrived in time?"

Again she nodded. She knew she must look like a fool but she could not help herself.

"Would you like a drink?" he asked. "I've some wine in my room."

Her mouth was exceptionally dry, and so she nodded again.

She saw him smile, and then he slipped back through the door, before returning with a decanter full of a dark red liquid and two glasses.

"You're nervous," he said. It wasn't a question, but she found herself compelled to answer it all the same.

"Yes."

He poured them both a glass of wine and placed hers on the dressing table, before perching on the edge of the bed with his.

"Nothing needs to happen tonight, if you don't wish it."

SHE LOOKED SO terrified he didn't even feel he could reach out and take her hand, as he had in the carriage. Somehow he thought that might make her even more uncomfortable. He had entered this room in anticipation of a potentially awkward wedding night, but he had not thought she would look quite so terrified.

In truth, he had never lain with an innocent before. The lovers he had taken had always been widows; women who knew exactly what they wanted, and what to expect.

He had never once had a partner who was not as enthusiastic as he was.

Her blue eyes met his, and he could tell she wanted to say something, although the words did not seem to be coming.

"The marriage will need to be, ah, consummated," he said, surprised at how difficult it was to broach the topic with someone who seemed to have so little knowledge about what to expect. "And do our best to produce an heir. But that does not need to be tonight…"

"Do I not appeal to you?" she asked, her voice unexpectedly strong.

His eyes widened in shock. "What on earth makes you think that?"

"I may be naive, Lord—Laurence. But I know that attraction plays a part in…in…"

"The marital act," Laurence provided, when she did not seem to be able to find the words—although he had never described it in such detached terms before.

"Yes. And that it is expected to occur on the wedding night. And that men…men desire this act more than women."

Laurence quirked his eyebrow. That had not always been his experience, but he supposed it was how many married couples viewed things.

"I have heard of your reputation," she said, her voice dropping low as though she was afraid someone might hear about his scandalous past. "So I can only surmise that you find me unattractive."

Laurence shook his head. "You are entirely wrong, Anastasia. I don't want you to feel pressured into something you are not prepared for…but I certainly find you attractive. And I would like to show you that women can desire this act just as much as men can."

# CHAPTER THIRTEEN

H E TOOK THE glass of wine from her and placed both back on the dressing table, before encircling her wrist with his fingers and pulling her towards him.

Her heart skittered and she was so nervous she almost pulled away—until he pressed his lips against hers.

Their first kiss. Her first kiss. It was soft at first, and yet it still took her breath away. She was consumed by the sandalwood scent of him, presumably from his soap, and the way he pulled her against him, her soft body melding against his solid frame.

One hand moved to pluck pins from her hair as his lips progressed from hers to her cheek, her earlobe, her neck…

She groaned, unable to help herself, as a white-hot heat shot through her from every point of her body where his lips grazed.

Was he uncommonly good at this? Or did every kiss make a lady feel like she was going to melt away to nothing?

She didn't even notice him maneuvering them both to the bed, until she was laying upon it, and his kisses moved to her collarbone, her décolletage…

Then he pulled down the shoulder of her dress, kissing every inch of skin that he bared, until she was writhing on the bed beneath him, desperate for *more.*

She pulled him closer, her fingers digging into his bare back. She hadn't even noticed him removing his shirt but it was gone, and his warm, strong body was pressing against hers as he kissed her senseless.

Her worries about what the night would entail disappeared as she lost the ability to think, simply giving into the pleasure he had awoken within her.

Having divested her of every item of clothing she had been wearing, he trailed kisses down her entire body, yet she could not find it in herself to be shocked or to try to cover up. She had not known that desire could feel like this. All-consuming, overwhelming, pulsing through her body.

"Please," she said with a groan, not knowing what she was begging for. He placed a kiss on the arch of her foot, then returned to her lips, as his fingers slid up her thigh and found the bud of nerves that made her cry out.

SHE WAS MORE sensual than he had ever imagined. He had kissed every inch of her creamy skin, delighting in turning it pink, before he returned to her lips, kissing her until he was breathless.

When he touched her for the first time, he found himself watching her face, thrilled to be giving her this first taste of desire. He was desperate to chase his own release and yet somehow teasing groans and gasps from Anastasia as his fingers moved between her legs was almost more pleasurable.

When he could bear the torturous delight no longer, he moved his hips over hers, and locked eyes with her momentarily. She gave him a shy smile, and his heart began to race.

This was not his first time, not by a long stretch—but this time it meant something. This time, it would seal their union as man and wife.

"It may hurt, for a moment," he said, not wanting to ruin the heady atmosphere, but also not wanting to shock her.

She simply leant forward and kissed him, as they became one.

She gasped and he froze, hating the thought of hurting her,

and with no experience to draw on when it came to an un-touched woman.

But when she opened her eyes, he saw the desire still there, and she squeezed her knees against his thighs, encouraging him to move.

He kissed her once more, rather surprised at the strength of the emotions filling him at this momentous moment, and her back arched and he gasped himself at the pleasure such a simple motion caused to shoot through his body.

They moved together, both chasing release, his lips pressed to her neck, her breath hot against his ear.

"Laurence…please…oh," she cried out, and she clung to him as his release took his breath away.

He lay beside her, holding her close, and it took a long time for his breathing to return to normal. He turned his head to look at her, and she blushed and smiled and nestled her head against his chest.

"Is there anything you need?" he asked, his mind rather scrambled at just how mind-blowing the encounter had been.

She shook her head and he felt it against his skin.

Had it been so good because she had been a virgin? Or because she was his wife? Because he'd lain with many women, and chased a lot of pleasure, but never before had it felt as intense.

He turned once more and absent-mindedly pressed a kiss to the top of her head, as exhaustion threatened to overwhelm him.

WHEN ANASTASIA WOKE up, she was alone. That in itself should not have been surprising; she'd been waking up alone every morning she could remember.

And yet she had always gone to bed alone then, too. Now she was a wife, and she had spent the night with her husband, and she had somehow expected that when she woke up, he would still be beside her.

But he was gone.

She rolled over and tucked the sheets tightly around her naked body. She had never slept naked before, but after they had lain together…well, she presumed she had fallen asleep without even thinking of redressing. Her cheeks flushed warm at the thought.

Had he donned his clothes again when he had left her room to go, presumably, back to his own? Had he waited for her to fall asleep and then snuck out? Or had he woken and decided he was in the wrong place?

The sound of birdsong and the light bluish tinge that crept through the curtains told her it must be the early hours of the morning. Maybe he had not been gone long. She reached out to run her hand down his side of the bed, but it was stone cold. So he had not left recently.

She blinked back unexpected tears and told herself she was merely emotional after a long and surprising day. She had not known what to expect on her wedding night…and it had been far more, far greater, than she could have ever imagined. It had changed her, she was sure. She rather thought if she looked in the mirror, she would see a different woman. Her name might have changed to Lady Walsham the previous day, but it had not been until the night—their wedding night—that she had truly become her.

It was foolish to feel sad. For why should she expect him to stay? Most grand houses that she knew of boasted a master bedroom with an adjoining chamber for the wife, so it seemed likely that most men and women of their station slept in separate beds.

It had always made sense before. Why would one wish to share a bed if there was no need? Why would one wish to be asleep, and so vulnerable, in the presence of another?

But that had been before. Now…now it felt very unnatural to be parted from him so soon after they had been joined together.

But she supposed it was the way it was going to be. And so

she closed her eyes and tried to get a little more sleep, so that she could look at things more clearly, with less sentimentality, in the full light of day.

LAURENCE TOSSED AND turned in his bed, the bed that had once been his father's, the bed that felt very large and empty.

It made no sense. He had never spent the night, in its entirety, with a woman. And he had never brought one to this house. So this bed had always been one he had slept in alone. It had made sense to leave Miss—Lady—Anastasia's bed once she had fallen asleep, even if he had found it surprisingly hard to slide her from his arms and pad out the door.

The whole night had been rather more successful and enjoyable than he had expected. She had looked so terrified when he had come to her chamber, and he had felt compelled to offer her an escape, if only temporarily. The marriage would need to be consummated, of course, and an heir hopefully conceived—but it didn't have to be that night. He could have waited.

But she hadn't wanted to. And then, in rather a surprising revelation, she had given in to passion in a way he had not expected. Their compatibility, in the bedchamber at least, had been apparent almost immediately. And the prospect of conceiving a child certainly was not an arduous thought, if the efforts were to be a repeat of that night.

But then why could he not sleep? It had been a long day, and a satisfying evening. He should have fallen immediately into a sated sleep that would take him through to the next morning. But he could not. Something didn't feel quite right—but he could not put his finger on what it was.

With a sigh, he turned over, facing the door that connected his room to his wife's, and wondered if her hair was still splayed out on the pillow as it had been when he had left.

# CHAPTER FOURTEEN

"OH—GOOD MORNING," THE timid voice said as Laurence entered the dining room. Anastasia was sitting at the far end of the table in a green day dress that seemed to make her red hair look all the more fiery. It was neatly pinned up around her crown, but in his mind it was loose and flowing like it had been the night before. A pang of desire shot through him, and he swallowed and tried to redirect his thoughts to something more suitable to this time of the morning.

"Good morning. Did you sleep well?" he asked as he took his seat. The newspaper had been placed next to his plate, as it always was when he was in the city, and he glanced down at it for a moment before looking back up at his wife.

"I—" she paused, frowned, and then continued. "It is always a little odd, sleeping somewhere new."

So she had not slept well either. Being in a new place could certainly explain her restlessness—but what reason could he put to his?

"Do you have any plans today?" Laurence asked, breaking the awkward silence. While the previous night had been a revelation, this morning he barely knew the woman sitting across from him. They had no common interests on which to converse, nor any knowledge of one another. He did not know what she liked to do when she was not socializing with the rest of the ton. They were strangers, bound together for the rest of their lives.

Their marriage had been so unexpected that he certainly *did* have plans for the day. He had an appointment with his man of business to discuss his estates, and he had planned to return to the country as soon as he felt he could—without seeing the ghost of his father everywhere. Although now, he presumed he would have to stay in London. Surely the new Lady Walsham would wish to see out the rest of the Season in the city.

He did not think he had the heart for socializing in the way he used to. It was hard to pretend that the grief was not there for an entire evening of cards or drinking or dancing. Of course, he had always had the option to lose himself in the arms of a woman, but now that was different, too. Not that every man remained entirely loyal to his wife, of course. And it wasn't exactly a topic they had discussed. Once they had provided the title with an heir, and were perhaps living life more separately, he was sure there would be other women once more. And perhaps Anastasia would take a lover. It was not uncommon for women who had done their duty to seek pleasure elsewhere. He ought to know—he had often been the one sharing such women's beds.

His brow furrowed, the thought of Anastasia with another man more distasteful than he expected. Well, all of that was for the future. For now, being faithful certainly seemed like the right thing to do. And so the city did not hold much interest for him.

But he didn't feel it would be fair to his young new wife to tear her away from everything and disappear into the quiet and solitude of the countryside so soon after they were wed.

He had been so lost in his thoughts that it had taken him a moment to realize that she was still deliberating over his rather simple question.

"I suppose…well…no. I have no plans."

Laurence nodded. Considering someone else's plans was all rather new to him. With the wedding being unexpected, he had not planned any sort of honeymoon, rather thinking that their lives would simply continue on as they had before they were wed.

"Well, feel free to use the carriage. And if you wish to make any purchases—new gowns or hats or gloves or what have you—just have them send the bill here. You're Lady Walsham now," he said with a smile. "Don't forget it."

He had hoped she would be cheered by the thought of having the freedom to do what she wished, to spend money how she liked, but her face simply fell, and she turned back to her breakfast.

ANASTASIA PICKED AT the fruits on her plate, not really having any appetite. *You're Lady Walsham now.* He obviously felt she needed to improve herself, to be worthy of the name. She had thought her gowns were acceptable, but clearly he wanted her to shop for new ones, befitting her station. Nerves about her new position filled her stomach, making it impossible to eat. Last night, everything had seemed so simple. Everything had seemed to fit.

And yet this morning, they were simply strangers who lived together, who had no idea of the other's needs or wants or interests.

She had rather hoped that they might leave London, at least for a while. Gossip about their match was sure to continue, and she would have preferred to be away from it. She also had no interest in seeing her brother, her only relative in the city. She was so hurt by his actions that she wasn't sure she could ever feel the same way about him. And besides, he was still in trouble, financially. He had made it clear that having a sister as a viscountess was something he thought could be useful to him, and she was sure it would not be long until he came looking for her aid.

And it was aid she did not wish to give.

But Lord Walsham...Laurence...did not suggest leaving the city. In fact, it seemed he planned to continue as he had before.

After breakfast, he collected his top hat and left with a cheery wave. No kiss, no sign of affection, nothing like the passion they had shared the previous night.

Anastasia wandered the townhouse, familiarizing herself with its many rooms. She glanced in at his study but closed the door quickly, feeling that she was trespassing. The pale blue parlor, however, felt more feminine, and with nothing else to do, she called for tea and sat and pondered.

He did seem to be carrying on as though nothing had changed. Did that mean he would continue with every aspect of his life? Her hand shook a little as she set the delicate bone china cup back on the saucer.

He was a well-known rake. It had not meant much to her—until the night before. Until they had shared such pleasure. The thought of him sharing that with another woman was painful, and it made her stomach churn even more than thoughts of being the viscountess. Would he continue to take lovers now that they were wed?

She knew, thanks to the gossips of the ton, that many men were not faithful to their wives. And of course, she'd had no discussion about expectations with Laurence—not before they were wed, and not now. She could not even imagine having such a conversation. Her cheeks burned red at the mere suggestion of it.

Theirs had not been a love match. So why would he think there was any need for him to abstain from taking other women to his bed?

She drank her tea, even though she felt queasy, and tried to put the image of his long, lithe body wrapped around a nameless, faceless other woman out of her head.

Such thoughts surely led to madness.

# CHAPTER FIFTEEN

THE PARLOR HAD become Anastasia's favorite room in the house. She had once again woken up alone in her bedchamber, and it made her want to leave the room as quickly as possible. She didn't understand why Laurence disappeared in the middle of the night, or how things could be so easy, so incredible between them when he came to her room after dark, and yet so awkward the following day.

This morning, he had been gone from the house before she had even sat down to breakfast. The butler, a tall, stately-looking man by the name of Johnson, had not known exactly where he had gone, just that he had taken a horse out a little after eight.

Was he purposefully avoiding her? Or did he just lead a busy life—one which he clearly had no plans to change despite being married? She drew comfort from the fact that he was always there at night. Well, as far as she knew, he was. When he left her room, she assumed he went to his own…

She sat and sipped tea in the light blue room, trying to ignore the voice in the back of her head that told her there was no law saying the relations she shared with her husband at night couldn't take place in the daytime, if he were continuing his dalliances with other women.

A knock on the parlor door drew her out of her maudlin thoughts, and she forced a smile as Johnson entered and bowed. "Mr. Carrington is here to see you, my lady." Johnson held out a silver dish, upon which lay a card—presumably Oliver's. The butler surely knew Oliver was her brother; butlers always knew far, far more than they were ever told. But Oliver had never been a guest in this house, and so clearly Johnson thought things ought to be done properly.

She considered, for a moment, telling Johnson to inform her brother that she was not in. Oliver was sure to know it was a lie, but being "not at home" to guests one did not wish to see was hardly a new phenomenon.

But then the staff would surely talk, or worse, her brother might get angry and cause a scene…

She was the Viscountess Walsham now. She did not wish to besmirch her own name, or that of her husband.

And so, even though she had no wish at all to see her brother, she nodded. "Thank you, Johnson. Please send him in. And could you ask Mrs. Yates for some more tea? This has gone quite cold."

With a bow of his head, Johnson disappeared to do as she asked, and Anastasia steeled herself for the entrance of her brother.

"Annie," he said with a broad smile, his arms open as if to embrace her. It was more friendly and affectionate than he had been with her in years, and for a moment she felt herself soften toward him. He was her brother, after all. The only relative she knew still alive.

Johnson frowned, as though disapproving of Oliver calling the Viscountess "Annie," before leaving to fetch the tea.

"Hello, Oliver," she said, standing to embrace him. "Are you well?" She had not seen him in the three weeks since she had married Laurence. It was probably the longest they had gone without seeing each other in their whole lives.

"So formal, dear sister. I am well enough. And you? You are positively blooming as the new Lady Walsham."

She sat, folding her hands in her lap, and he took an armchair opposite her.

"I am well, thank you," she said, even though she wasn't

entirely sure it was true. Physically she was well enough, that was for sure. But the confusing nature of her relationship with her husband—the closeness they shared at night, and then the distance between them during the day—was making her feel rather seasick.

She supposed she was being rather formal. But she did not know how to be with him anymore. He had behaved in a way she had never thought possible, and she did not know whether she would ever be able to forgive him.

"You haven't been seen at any events," Oliver commented. "I didn't know if you were perhaps taking a honeymoon, or whether you are ill... Is your husband not at home?"

Anastasia shook her head. "I am afraid he is out at present." She did not give any further details—because she could not. Although even if she had known where Laurence was, she wasn't sure she would have told Oliver. It didn't feel entirely wise to share information with him; didn't seem like he could be trusted.

"Well, I'm sorry to have missed him," Oliver said, although Anastasia thought he looked anything but. "I trust he is treating you well?"

*And would you care if he wasn't?* Anastasia nearly asked him, but she stopped herself at the last moment. She rather wanted to know the answer, but it would not do either of them any good to start an argument now. Neither of them could change the fact that he had tried to marry her off to Baron Brett without her permission.

"Yes, thank you. The viscount and I are very happy."

Another answer that wasn't entirely true. They were not unhappy. But they didn't know each other well enough to be happy. ...At least she didn't think so. But she wasn't sure. She didn't know where he was, or what he spent his time doing. And while at night she felt a connection, in the day she felt so utterly alone...

But she wasn't going to admit any of that to Oliver.

"Excellent. So everything turned out for the best, then. No

hard feelings all around."

Did he mean that she shouldn't have hard feelings toward him, for his actions that night? Or that he held no hard feelings toward her, for ruining his plan?

Again, she didn't think it was a good idea to ask.

"As wonderful as your new marriage is, it has left me in rather a difficult situation."

"Oh?" Anastasia said, her heart sinking. So here it was—the reason he was here. She had hoped, perhaps naively, that he had just wished to see her. Just missed her. Perhaps felt bad about his behavior.

But it did not seem that that was the case.

"As you are aware, I owe some money. To Baron Brett…among others."

Anastasia gritted her teeth.

"And now that you are married to a man of such means, I need you to help me."

Anastasia stiffened. "I cannot ask Laurence for money, so soon after we have wed. It's not right."

"Of course you can. He's as rich as Croesus—he won't even notice it. Just tell him you wish to buy something nice for yourself. New dresses or—"

"Why should I lie?" Anastasia asked with a raised eyebrow. "And besides, he's already said I can purchase gowns. But he just asked for the bill to be sent to him. So there would be no reason for me to have any money from him. Not like that."

Oliver sighed, as if she were saying something very stupid. She'd seen this reaction many times before. As much as she had always loved her brother, and wanted a close relationship with him, he had not always seemed to like her.

"I cannot have the viscount knowing the extent of my financial…affairs. It would reflect poorly on the Carrington name, as would me defaulting on these payments. You don't want that, do you?" He smiled as though he were confident he knew exactly what she wanted—when in fact he knew nothing of the sort.

"I am no longer a Carrington," she said, holding her head up high. "What makes you think I am so concerned with what becomes of the name?" Her anger toward her brother gave her the confidence to speak so, but when he gave her a withering glare, she found herself shrinking back. She had always struggled to stand up to Oliver.

"My, my, you are an ungrateful girl," he said, crossing his legs and leaning forward. "You may no longer be a Carrington, but I know you. And I know you would not want Father's name—our father's legacy—to be ruined."

*Ruined because of your gambling,* she thought to herself, but she didn't quite dare to say it. He had that angry glint in his eye that warned she should not push him any further. While he had not lost control physically in a few years, as a child she had certainly been on the wrong side of him when she had pushed him too far and he had responded with a stinging slap instead of stinging words. She hoped he had better control of his anger now, as an adult…but she did not really wish to test it.

"You need to find a way to fix this problem that you created by running off into the dark walk with Lord Walsham like a harlot. I don't care how you find the money, but I need you to get it."

"But I don't—" Anastasia began.

"Enough." Oliver raised his voice and stood to emphasize his point. He reached forward and grabbed her arm, his fingers tightening around her wrist. "I need five hundred pounds. As soon as possible. And remember—not a word to your husband about the real reason. Or else."

It was surely an empty threat, for she could not think of anything he could really do if she did not comply. And yet the way he looked at her and held onto her struck fear into her very soul, and she found herself nodding.

His grip on her wrist loosened, and a smile returned to his face. "Good girl. Now, I'll see myself out, shall I? I'm sure you're very busy, now you're a great lady."

# CHAPTER SIXTEEN

LAURENCE STEPPED OUT onto the sunny London street from the office his lawyer kept at the end of Chancery Lane. He had wanted to update his will, now that he was wed, just to make sure Anastasia would be provided for and would never have to return to her brother if something happened to him. He did not like Oliver Carrington, and he never wanted her at his mercy again.

He glanced up and down the busy street and paused at the sight of a flash of red hair in the crowd.

He had always found redheads attractive, but now he always seemed to be checking whether they were Anastasia—although there was no reason why she would be in this part of London right now.

But still, he paused—and that was his downfall.

The redhead spotted him too and made her way toward him. By the time he realized it was very definitely not Anastasia, she had already set her sights on him.

He groaned inwardly, though he tried to keep his expression neutral. He certainly did not want to cause a scene or set off the London gossips.

Lady Frindley cut through the crowd, and he had no choice but to stand and wait for her to reach him.

"Lord Walsham," she said with an icy smile on her lips, nonetheless. "Well met. Why, I have not seen you since your charming little wedding. How is the new Lady Walsham?"

It felt wrong to discuss Anastasia with her, like he was opening up his wife to some evil force, although he did not truly understand the feeling. Lady Frindley had never done anything particularly cruel or nasty, as far as he knew. She was just rather too persistent…

"She is well, thank you," Laurence said. "And I trust you are well also?"

"Exceedingly so," Lady Frindley said, her tongue darting between her teeth. "I wonder, might you care to take a walk around Russell Square with me?"

"Thank you, but I'm afraid I must decline. I must be getting back."

He had absolutely no wish to take a walk with Lady Frindley, and he was sure she knew that. Indeed, why would she ask him unless she hoped for some reconciliation between the two—a continuation of the love affair they once enjoyed?

But that would not be happening. Even if Laurence did return to his rakish ways at some point in the future—although it was a scenario he was finding harder and harder to imagine—he could not see a situation in which he would ever rekindle things with Lady Frindley. For one, he never continued a dalliance for longer than a couple of months. And secondly, she had grown far too tenacious for his liking. He always liked to make a clean break and had always made sure that any lady in his life was aware of the fleeting nature of their romance.

And somehow, Lady Frindley was the first who had been unsatisfied with the way things had ended. She had wanted more—and he had not been willing to give more.

He had never thought he had any more to give… and yet, now he was married.

And he was reevaluating that belief.

Lady Frindley's smile tightened. "Well then, perhaps I shall just have to pay a call on you in the near future. And meet your lovely wife properly, of course. I'm sure she and I would have plenty to discuss."

Laurence swore in his head. She had him, and he was sure she knew it. A walk with her now would certainly be preferable to her paying him a call, sitting and talking to Anastasia about God knew what. Not that he had done anything wrong—he didn't think. His relationship with Lady Frindley had been well before he and Anastasia married. But still, he rather thought that the bold widow would make his new young wife rather uncomfortable.

And he really did not want that.

"Perhaps a short walk would be possible," he said, his grip tightening on the cane he carried—one his father had always had with him.

"Excellent!" Lady Frindley said, threading her arm through his and leading him in the direction of the park.

He bristled at how close she was and struggled to understand how, less than a year earlier, he had found her so attractive. She had driven him wild, and yet now, if anything, her presence irritated him. He looked down at her as they walked; it wasn't her appearance that had changed, and nor did he think her personality was particularly different than it had been when they were together.

It was surely he who had changed…

But was it the death of his father, his new title, or Anastasia that had changed everything so completely?

"And how is marriage treating you?" Lady Frindley asked, her soft bosom pressing against his arm as they walked. He felt decidedly uncomfortable and hoped he could extricate himself from the walk as quickly as possible.

"Very well, thank you," he said without hesitation. And it was. Perhaps he wished he understood her a little more, knew her a little better—but there was no doubting that they had a strong connection. He was confident that many marriages that had been planned much more thoroughly than theirs did not enjoy such strong chemistry as he and Anastasia did.

"I must admit I was surprised at your choosing to marry—and an innocent girl with no knowledge of how to be a viscountess at that."

Laurence bristled at her negative attitude toward Anastasia but decided it was better to keep things as friendly as possible.

"Well, the heart wants what the heart wants," he said.

She stopped suddenly and looked up at him. "So this was a love match, was it?"

"I—"

He did not like to lie, and the marriage had certainly not been a love match. But there was no denying that his heart was somewhat involved now, even if he wasn't sure it could be called love. He certainly cared for her.

"Lady Walsham and I are very happy," he said in the end, even though it didn't really answer the question.

"I see," Lady Frindley said, and he wanted to ask her exactly what it was she thought she saw, but he did not wish to prolong the conversation any more than was necessary.

"You know," Lady Frindley said, continuing to walk with her arm tightly in his, "I was disappointed when our arrangement came to an end last Season."

"I apologize. As you know, my father—"

She nodded. "Yes, yes, it was extremely sad. And I understood your need to grieve, to leave the city for a time. But when you returned..."

"Things had changed, Caroline," he said firmly. "I'm sorry that that was the case. You knew that our relationship was unlikely to last for long. I am sorry if I hurt you, but—"

She gave a laugh, which did not sound entirely convincing.

"It's not that you hurt me, Laurence. Gosh, you do think highly of yourself. It's simply that the arrangement seemed to benefit us both, and I saw no need—indeed, I *see* no need—for it to come to an end."

"I am married now." It seemed like an obvious thing to point out, but the lady didn't seem to understand that meant their relationship could not continue. Perhaps for some people, marriage was no object but somehow, with Anastasia—things were different.

Lady Frindley shrugged and laughed again, but this time it sounded colder. "We both know that doesn't need to mean anything. Why, even before Lord Frindley died, we both had our dalliances. It made for a more successful marriage, I daresay."

In the past, Laurence rather thought he might've agreed with her. Having other interests—indeed, other people—outside of the marriage would surely allow it to flourish.

But it was different in reality. It was different with Anastasia. Thinking of her in bed with another man made him feel physically sick, and the thought of taking another woman to his bed held no appeal whatsoever. He only wanted Anastasia. It had certainly not been what he had expected, but it was the way things had turned out.

"We could carry on as we were," Lady Frindley continued. "No one would have to know. *She* wouldn't have to know. I can be very discreet…and I'm confident I can please you in ways a naive little chit like her never could."

He pulled his arm from hers, anger making his blood boil. It was one thing to suggest they continue their liaison, but quite another to insult Anastasia in such a vile way—and in public too, where they might be overheard.

"For the final time—no. We had an enjoyable Season together, and now it has come to an end. Please accept that, Caroline—and do not contact me again."

And with that, he turned on his heel and stalked out of the park toward home, hoping that he had not made a grave error in making an enemy of Lady Frindley.

# CHAPTER SEVENTEEN

"JOHNSON SAID YOUR brother was here," Laurence said over their dinner of pork chops that evening.

It still felt rather formal between them when they sat like this at opposite ends of the large dining table. In fact, it always felt formal—until the night, when they were alone. Then, everything felt rather easy. He struggled to hide his distaste when he mentioned her brother. What little he had seen of Oliver Carrington before he had met Anastasia had not endeared the man to him, but his behavior that night in Vauxhall Gardens had rather disgusted him.

He had treated his sister with no care whatsoever for her feelings or wishes, and Laurence was not sorry to have missed his visit.

Anastasia's reaction surprised him, however. Her eyes widened as though she had been caught out, and then she nodded.

"Was there a reason for his visit?" Laurence asked, his curiosity piqued.

Anastasia put a piece of pork in her mouth and spent a very long time chewing it—certainly far longer than the seconds it needed.

Laurence waited somewhat impatiently, feeling as though she were keeping something from him. Had her brother caused a scene? Laurence wasn't sure what he could have an issue with now, and if there had been some drama, he was sure his staff would have informed him.

"He just…hasn't seen me since we were wed."

"So he was checking to see that you were well?"

She nodded quickly. "Yes. Yes, that was it."

Laurence did not feel comfortable enough in their relationship to challenge her, even though he was sure she was lying.

"Did you have a productive day?" she asked, and his mind flickered back to the encounter with Lady Frindley, and the uncomfortable conversation that he would certainly not be repeating to Anastasia.

"Yes, yes, quite productive," he said, looking down at his newspaper.

ANASTASIA HATED HOW awkward and forced conversation seemed between them in the daylight hours. She knew why she was struggling to fill the silence, tonight, at least—because there was more to her brother's visit, and she could not disclose it to him.

But why, when asked, did he not elaborate on his day? He disappeared from the house for most of the daylight hours, and yet she had no idea what he was doing.

Was he seeing another woman? Or *women*, even? She wished she had the guts to ask him, for the thought taunted her whenever she allowed her mind to wander in that direction.

Later, as she lay in his arms—the one moment in the day where everything felt right in the world—she closed her eyes and tried to sleep.

Unusually, sleep would not come. While she often woke in the early hours to find herself alone and struggled to get back to sleep, falling asleep after they had made love was never normally a problem.

Tonight, however, her thoughts turned to her brother's demands. She flexed her wrist, remembering the tight grip he'd had on it, even though there was no mark to show for it. He couldn't really hurt her if she did not comply, could he? They did not even live together anymore. She could simply refuse him entry.

But he was right about one thing: she didn't want to see her family's name ruined, even if her name was now Walsham and not Carrington. And her husband was richer than she could have ever imagined being. He wouldn't notice the money...and if Oliver had a clean slate, perhaps he would stop acting so foolishly.

How was she to get the money? If she could not tell Laurence what it was for, then she could not ask him outright for it. She was a terrible liar, and he would surely know if she tried to deceive him.

If there had been something from her own possessions that she could sell, from before they were wed, then she would have done so, but Oliver had sold any family heirlooms of worth long ago, and her dresses would not fetch the sums he required. Her eyes wandered over to the jewelry box on the dressing table, which she could just see in the glowing embers of the dying fire. The jewels belonging to the Viscountess Walsham. That was her, after all. If there was one thing she could sell that would not be noticed, then maybe this whole mess could go away.

Guilt at what she felt she must do gnawed at her stomach, and she almost turned in order to remove the jewelry box from her line of sight, when she remembered that Laurence was still there, his arms wrapped around her, his bare form pressed against her back.

She sighed and leaned back into him, the silence of the room disturbed only by the ticking clock on the mantel.

How long was it until he would leave?

They had been married for a month and had spent every night together, and yet still he left once she was asleep. Without a word. It had not been discussed, and she was not brave enough to broach the topic, and so she did not truly understand why he left—she just knew that he did.

And that she wished he would stay.

Time ticked on, and she tried not to think about her brother, tried to enjoy this time where she felt content in her marriage, in her life. It wasn't just the sexual relations, although they were more earth-shattering than she could have ever imagined. No, it was the closeness, the feeling that there were only the two of them in the world, that he knew her better than anyone else.

Of course, she knew that wasn't true. In the cold light of day, it was clear that their connection did not extend past the bedchamber. But in the quiet of the night, she could persuade herself that it did.

She felt his body stiffen, and his arm slide away from her. Did he think she was asleep? Or had the time come for him to leave, whether or not she was awake?

She nearly let him go without a word, nearly pretended she was asleep in order to avoid an awkward conversation.

But she didn't want him to go. And if he was going to, she thought, she at least deserved to know why.

"Do you have to leave?" she asked, her voice ringing out in the still room, surprising herself by her own boldness.

Behind her, his body froze.


"I THOUGHT YOU were asleep," Laurence said, feeling like he had been caught doing something wrong. He left every night, and she had never said a word. He had presumed it was what she wanted, and that had made it easier to keep leaving, even though he had often imagined staying in her embrace, perhaps waking to the sunlight reaching the curtains and making love once more as the day truly began.

"I know. But do you *have* to leave?"

It was hard to read her emotions without being able to see her face. He did not know how to answer her. Of course, there was no reason why he needed to leave, other than it being the way things were done. The way he had always done it, anyway.

"No… I suppose I don't need to leave," he said, frozen

somewhere between lying down and sitting up, not sure if she wanted him to stay or if she was merely questioning him.

She nodded her head, and he wished he could see those blue eyes, to try to read what she was really thinking.

"Stay." It was one word, delivered as both a command and a request.

One word that made it clear what she wanted—in that moment, at least.

And so he lay back down, and pulled her bare body back against his, and allowed himself to close his eyes and sleep in his wife's bed for the first time.

When he awoke, Laurence thought he was dreaming. His arousal—which was always present when he woke up these days—was pressed against the soft form of his slumbering wife. It was a dream he'd had many times before, and yet this morning, it felt different. He could tell he was not in his own bed, for one, and he did not immediately wake up, as he so annoyingly seemed to do in his dreams just when things were getting good.

He pressed his nose to her hair and inhaled the floral smell that he presumed came from her soap. And then he felt her stiffen in his arms, clearly awakening herself.

This was no dream.

She pressed her soft behind against him and he groaned, unable to control himself. He had lost count now of the number of times they had made love in this bed, but never in the morning, with the sun streaming in through a gap in the curtains.

Anastasia rolled over, and he could not help but beam at the sight of her, red hair loose and splayed across the pillow, her eyes barely awake and yet already full of desire.

She kissed him first but he responded enthusiastically, his tongue meeting hers as his hands slid to her soft hips, pulling her tight against his arousal.

How did he still want her so desperately, after weeks of marriage?

Her hands slid up his chest, and then she swung her leg across him, straddling him as they continued to kiss. His fingers entangled in her hair, pulling her closer, always desperate for more of her.

Was this the high some men got from gambling or drink? He found himself constantly thinking about her, and he never had his fill.

ANASTASIA WAS SURE her cheeks were burning red, but she didn't care. He had stayed the whole night, and she had awoken in his arms, and now she wanted to take control of the desire for him that coursed through her veins.

She was rather surprised by her own boldness when she wriggled her hips and took him inside of her. She pulled away from their kiss slightly, wanting to see his face, and it was to her satisfaction that his eyes were wide and his mouth slack. He groaned, and she moved, her whole body lighting up from that point of connection. She moved again, chasing the pleasure that had immediately begun to build, and he gripped one of her hips with a broad hand and began to rock his hips in time with hers. His other hand caressed up her body until he was holding the weight of her breast in his palm. His thumb brushed across her nipple and she cried out, her whole body tensing as her release washed over her, sudden and explosive.

Moments later, he cried out, and Anastasia lay against him, her breath coming in pants, his chest heaving.

"I could happily wake up like that for the rest of my life," he murmured into her ear, and she laughed in spite of her breathlessness and luxuriated in the joy of that moment, lying in his arms.

# CHAPTER EIGHTEEN

WHEN SHE WOKE up to find blood on the crisp white sheets of her large bed, Anastasia was mortified—and rather pleased that, although Laurence had stayed the night, he had already left to go about whatever business it was that he did in the day.

Her bleeding was so irregular that she never quite knew when to expect it. She did not think this was the case for all women, but she did not know any well enough to have a frank conversation with them about such things. Her own mother had died before her menses had begun, and her maid Elsie had been the one to explain them to her, when she had thought she was surely dying.

But normally, she noticed the signs before the bleeding began—the tenderness in her breasts, the dragging feeling in her stomach. This time, it had either been symptomless, or she had been too distracted to notice, for it had come upon her as rather a shock.

Did Laurence know about such things? How could she possibly speak to him about it without dying of embarrassment? But she would have to say something, for they had lain together every night since they were wed, and he would surely expect a reason to be given if she refused him.

She stripped the bed sheets herself, embarrassed to let the maid do so, even though of course she would know what had happened. It was different this time, in this new house, with staff she barely knew. She was once again struck by how alone she felt. The only time she felt complete was at night, when Laurence came to her, when he held her in his arms, when they spent the night with their bodies wrapped around one another. Tears pricked at her eyes as she realized that she would be even more alone now—for the next few days, at least. For there would be no reason for him to come to her room, since he could not lie with her.

Would he find another woman to lie with, while she was…indisposed?

She felt sick at the very thought. All day, as she completed embroidery and practiced the pianoforte, she fretted about how to tell him, about how he would react, about what words she would use. She practiced the conversation in her head, feeling ridiculous and yet blushing even when speaking in her mind to the imaginary Laurence.

She had never discussed such a topic in front of a man, of course. Her brother and father would never have raised the subject. Somewhere in the recesses of her mind, she remembered her maid telling her that it had something to do with bearing children, but she could not quite remember the details.

How she wished she had paid more attention. Or that she had a female in her life she could turn to, to ask the questions that no one else could answer.

But alas, she was alone.


ANASTASIA HAD BARELY set foot in Laurence's study since they had been wed, but that night she decided to go and find him there, rather than waiting for him to join her in her chamber. It seemed like it would be an easier conversation to have when she were not undressed and ready for bed.

The door was closed, and she knocked and waited for him to call her in, nerves bubbling in her stomach. Was it normal to feel nervous to speak to one's husband?

"Enter," his deep voice called, and she turned the knob and pushed the door open.

He was sitting behind the dark mahogany desk, a sheaf of papers splayed out before him, but he looked up when she entered and immediately smiled. That look sent a flutter through Anastasia's whole body, a flutter which made her more annoyed that her bleeding had started.

"I hoped we could talk," Anastasia rushed out, as he stood and offered her a chair before the fire.

"Of course." He took the seat next to her, instead of the one he had been occupying behind his desk, and looked at her expectantly, his hands open on his lap, his knees almost touching hers.

"I can't... I don't think... I mean..." All the words she had planned to say seemed to abandon her as she sat beneath his warm gaze, and she wasn't sure if it helped or hindered when he reached out and took her hand in his.

"YOU NEEDN'T BE so nervous around me," he said, feeling rather guilty that she did not seem more confident in his presence after a month of marriage. But then, was he more confident in hers? He wasn't scared of her by any means, but he didn't find he knew what to say to her. What to share. With other women, before they had wed, he had always felt more...confident. Not in the bedroom, for there, things between him and his wife were exceptional. But outside of it...

If he thought about it more, he supposed he had never spent much time out of the bedroom with any of the women he had known. Pillow talk he could do, but the conversation of a relationship, day in, day out? That, it seemed, he found harder.

But still. He did not want his wife quaking before him when she had something to tell him. That was no good. The instinct to take her hand came naturally, and he squeezed the soft, warm flesh gently, asking again, "What is bothering you, love?"

The term of endearment had slipped out rather unplanned,

and although he noticed himself saying it, he did not think making an issue of it was the right thing to do. Why shouldn't he call his wife "love"?

She swallowed, and raised her eyes from the floor to meet his. "I... I cannot lie with you tonight," she said in a shaky whisper.

"Oh," Laurence said, not letting go of her hand. He smiled. "That's fine, of course. You don't need to apologize or look so worried. Are you well?"

It didn't seem right that disappointment was his first emotion. They had made love every single night since they were married. It wasn't like he had not had his fill—except he never seemed to feel like he had. It was like he couldn't get enough of her. He would never have lain with a woman every single night before Anastasia. And he knew enough from the wry comments his friends and fellow peers made to know that it was not common for a husband and wife to make love every single night.

It was certainly fair that she wanted a night off. Perhaps he had been rather unfair in his expectations, especially considering she had been a virgin on their wedding night. Not that she had complained...but he now worried that she had been too afraid to do so. And since he had started staying all night, sometimes their bodies had found one another in the early hours of the morning, and they had made love then, too.

"I hope I have not...expected too much of you," Laurence said, feeling a little sick at the realization that she had perhaps not been the willing participant he had thought she was. Her reactions had seemed genuine, her pleasure as explosive as his...but maybe he'd been reading her all wrong.

Her face turned as red as her hair, and she shook her head. "No, I..." She didn't seem able to find the words. "It is not anything you have done, or a lack of... wanting to," she said, and Laurence allowed a small smile to cross his lips. *Well, that was a relief.*

"I simply... cannot. Not for a few days..." Her eyes met his and widened slightly, as if willing him to understand her meaning, and suddenly it became clear.

He was not used to women as shy or unsure as his dear wife. "Ah. Your monthly bleeding? I see. I had wondered…" He shook his head. He had not really thought about the possibility that she could already be with child, except when he had fleetingly realized that they had been married for over a month with no cessation in their activities. Not that he would have minded continuing, but he doubted that would be something Anastasia would want.

But no, she was making it clear that she was not with child—although he did not think that had been her intention in visiting him in his study.

"Mine have never been monthly," she said in a whisper, as though she were afraid someone would overhear her. Laurence nodded, wanting to put her at ease. He did understand now why she had felt so awkward about the conversation, although it seemed like a topic that a husband and wife ought to be able to discuss, since it was so pertinent to the act of procreation, which was the reason for marriage in the first place.

"I understand that is the case for some women. But you do know…" He paused, wondering how much she had been told. On their wedding night, she certainly seemed to have not been told many details about what to expect. But he supposed she had no woman in her life to fill that role. "When you are with child, the bleeding will stop. For the nine months that you carry the baby. It is a sign—usually the first sign, I believe—that a woman is with child."

LAURENCE STAYED LATE in his study that night, nursing a single glass of whiskey. For the last month, he had retired to bed far earlier than usual, but he found himself loath to go to bed alone.

How quickly he had become accustomed to spending every night with his wife. He wondered if she felt the same way.

He swirled the amber liquid around the bottom of his glass.

Earlier, for a moment, he had wondered if Anastasia was with child—if their certainly frequent efforts at conceiving had been successful in their very first month as husband and wife.

She was not...and he found his feelings about that were rather mixed. If she had been pregnant, it would have been another step along the way to fulfilling his vow to his father.

But he wasn't sure he was ready to be a father just yet. He thought of the way he had looked up to his own father and wondered whether a child of his could ever look up to him in the same way. Had he done enough yet to make a child proud? So far in his life, he had mainly lived for his own enjoyment, creating a reputation that followed him around.

He also thought it might be rather nice to have a little more time just him and Anastasia. He did not feel that they really knew each other that well yet. Adding a child into the mix would certainly complicate things, and so perhaps it would not be so terrible if it took a little longer to conceive.

He had married in order to continue the family name and to save Miss Carrington's reputation. But that did not mean they could not get a little more out of the marriage, did it?

She had looked so unsure when she had come to speak to him that he had felt guilty. He rather thought he needed to get to know her better—during the daylight hours.

# CHAPTER NINETEEN

ANASTASIA COULD NOT ignore the gnawing sense of guilt as she left the house with the silver necklace in her reticule. She had tried her best to ascertain, through the staff, that it was not a sentimental piece—but she couldn't be totally sure.

And while it did belong to her, she supposed, selling it did not feel right.

She had no idea how else she was going to get the money her brother needed. It would just be this once, she told herself. She would pawn it and hopefully be able to find a way to get it back. Perhaps she could save up the pin money Laurence gave her and repurchase it. Or maybe when Oliver was in a better position financially, she could persuade him to repay her.

"Anastasia?"

She was surprised to hear her husband's voice in the hallway at this time of day, and she turned around, feeling like she'd been caught doing something she shouldn't.

"Laurence! I did not know you were at home." He normally left after breakfast, occasionally returned for lunch, but was always back in time for dinner. She wasn't sure where he went all day, or who he saw, but it was the first morning since they had wed that he had sought her out at a time other than a mealtime.

Of course, it would be at a time when she wanted to leave the house unnoticed.

"Since the weather is so fine, I wondered if you would care to take a walk with me?"

Anastasia felt the expression on her face freeze. It was the first time he had reached out to spend more time with her outside the bedroom. And she wanted to say yes—but she needed to visit the pawnshop. She needed to get the money and to divest herself of the necklace as quickly as possible.

"I—I'm afraid I have plans today," she said, and she thought she saw his face fall a little.

"Oh. I see. Anything interesting?"

For the life of her, Anastasia could not think of a lie to tell him. The truth was that she spent her days doing very little of interest. She often stayed at home, reading or making sure everything was running smoothly in the house—although, to be honest, the house had been run for so long without a mistress that the housekeeper, Mrs. Yates, was perfectly capable and content to do so without instruction.

But it gave Anastasia something to do to fill the long days when Laurence was out. She would have preferred to be in the countryside, where she could while away her days out in nature, but it seemed Laurence had a preference for staying in London.

"I… I promised my brother I'd call upon him," she said eventually, although it was certainly too early for her brother to be receiving visitors, if he had been socializing the night before—which he generally always had been.

He wasn't really the right name to mention, either; his name clearly irritated Laurence, and she was sure he wondered why she would want to spend time with a man who treated her so poorly, even if he was her brother.

And he didn't even know the half of it.

But his was the only name that came to mind, and so she would just have to pretend it was true.


LAURENCE WAS SURE she was lying. He didn't know how he knew, but there was just something that made him suspicious. What he didn't know was why she was lying. Her brother was distasteful enough company—but was she seeing someone he would approve of even less? Or did she simply not wish to spend time with him? He had to admit, it rather smarted to be turned down when he had wanted to get to know her better.

She shifted her weight between her feet, avoiding his eye, and he wondered why she was so keen to go.

"Well, I won't keep you," he said with a shrug. "Perhaps we can take that walk another time."

"Yes, yes, perhaps," she said as she rushed out the door.

Laurence went to sit in his study, for it seemed like the natural thing to do, even though he had cleared his day of all work in order to try to get to know his wife a little better. It was too early for anything stronger, so he called for tea and sat staring out the window as he drank it.

Where was she going? And why did she not want him to know?

An uncomfortable thought prickled at his mind. Could it be that she was meeting with another man? After all, they had not known each other well before marrying, and perhaps she had been secretly courting someone.

But then wouldn't she have married that other man, when it became imperative that she wed?

There certainly ought not to have been a need for her to be betrothed to Baron Brett.

He did not like the thought of his wife with another man. And not just because she was his, and another man had no right. No, he also hated the thought of the passionate woman he knew laying with someone else. For another man to see that side of her—the side that he had thought was only for him.


It FELT STRANGE to visit her family home. She had not thought about the fact that she had not returned in the weeks since she had been wed, and it only dawned on her how long it had been as she stood on the stoop and knocked on the familiar front door.

When the butler opened the door, his face broke into a smile at the sight of her.

"Miss C—Lady Walsham. How lovely to see you." He bowed his head, and she smiled, her heart warming at being so fondly remembered.

"It's lovely to see you, too. I trust you are well?"

"Yes, thank you, my lady." It felt very strange getting used to the change in title when addressed by someone who had known her for so many years as Miss Carrington.

"And I hope you and the viscount are well too?"

"We are, thank you. Is my brother home?" She did not wish to be rude, but she was keen to complete her task and then leave the house. While it had felt like home for many years—now she did not feel entirely welcome. The money from the pawned necklace burned a hole in her pocket, and she wished to be rid of it and to return to the life she was now leading.

Laurence had asked her to go for a walk that morning. Perhaps, if she were home before the air grew too cool, he would still wish to walk that afternoon.

It felt like a step in the right direction toward gaining a deeper understanding of one another—one which did not begin and end in the bedchamber.

"Yes, my lady. If you would like to wait in the parlor, I shall inform him of your arrival."

She followed him in, feeling like a guest in the home she had run around in as a child. The parlor looked the same as always, although perhaps a little less used. It had been a room that she had primarily made use of, and so it had always been her books on the coffee table, her letters at the bureau. Now the room felt like it had lost its soul. She supposed it would be unlikely to be used regularly until Oliver married.

One day, she presumed, there would be a Mrs. Carrington who would sit in this parlor and pour tea and entertain, just as their mother had once done.

If Oliver hadn't gambled the house away by then.

Anastasia tried to dismiss the uncharitable thoughts. She was helping him now so that he could start fresh, so that he could put these debts behind him and move on. It was awful to think that he might just start over. And she meant to make it clear to him that she would not help him out every time he got into trouble. She would not and could not take money from her husband and lie to him all the time.

She heard Oliver's heavy tread on the stairs and wondered if he would berate the butler for showing her in before checking whether he was at home. Of course, that would be the normal way of doing things—but she supposed the butler did not think that her brother would wish to turn her away if he were indeed present.

Although he had been working for Oliver long enough to know of his changeable moods.

When he entered the parlor, there was a smile on her brother's face, and she immediately felt a little more at ease. She supposed he had guessed that she was here to help him, and that was why he was being friendly—but it always made things easier if he was in a good mood. She had spent many years of her life treading on eggshells around him, and she only realized the toll it had taken on her now that she had been removed from his presence. The air felt lighter and easier to breathe when she was not around him all the time.

What a terrible thing to think about one's own family. She hated to think what her father would have made of the relationship between his two children now. She did not think he had ever seen the side of Oliver that she knew all too well. She hoped he had not. She would feel happier knowing he had gone to his grave unaware that his son and heir could be such a bully.

"Anastasia!" he exclaimed, embracing her before taking a seat opposite her. "How lovely to see you again. Shall I call for some tea?"

Anastasia shook her head. "I can't stay long. I've brought the money you need."

His beady eyes lit up.

"I knew you'd figure out a way to help me," he said with a smile. "And Lord Walsham doesn't—"

Anastasia shook her head.

"He doesn't know about your debt, and he doesn't know that I've taken any money. And I'd like it to stay that way. Because this is only happening once—you must change your ways."

"Yes, yes, of course."

# CHAPTER TWENTY

WHEN ANASTASIA ARRIVED home, feeling lighter for having fulfilled her task, she went looking for Laurence. The weather was still pleasant, and she thought they might take that walk—even though she kept thinking how much nicer it would be to take a walk in the countryside, rather than in the stuffy city.

But Laurence was nowhere to be found. She checked his study, where he usually was, and the parlor and the great hall too. Then she asked his valet, whom she happened to catch in the hallway.

"He went out, my lady. About an hour ago—and he said he might be back late."

Anastasia felt her face fall. How she had hoped that they could push forward with the steps he had taken toward spending more time together that morning. But now he wasn't here. And he was going to be back late.

Where was he?

She tried not to think about it. Instead, she would make a plan—a plan for the following day. Hopefully, they could begin to get to know each other a little better, even after several weeks of marriage.

When she had made her plan, eaten her supper and taken a bath, and he was still not home, she found she could not shut out her thoughts any longer. Where was he—and who was he with?

In the whole time they had been married, he had never spent

the night away, and yet now she found herself getting ready for bed knowing that he was not home.

Was he seeking company elsewhere, because she had told him of her bleeding, and that she was indisposed? She supposed she had expected him to stay in his own bedchamber, but she had not expected him not to come home at all.

Time ticked on, and she sat at the window, looking out onto the moonlit street, anger building within her. He was making a fool of her by staying away overnight, and angry tears pooled in her eyes, distorting her view of the street.

The clock downstairs struck midnight, and still she did not hear his boots on the stairs, or his movements in the adjoining bedchamber.

As she climbed into bed, sorrow making her heart ache, she had the terrible thought that perhaps something had happened to him. What if he was hurt? Maybe his carriage had overturned, or he had been attacked by highwaymen? That would be even worse than him consorting with some other woman.

When she eventually slipped into a fitful sleep, having prayed for his safe return, her dreams were filled with disturbing images of crashed carriages and guns and blood.

The morning could not come quickly enough.

HAVING ONLY RETURNED in the early hours of the morning, Laurence had not seen Anastasia since the previous day, when she had left to go on her mysterious errand. He had not told her he was going, for when he had seen her, he hadn't known he was. The arrival of the letter detailing the leak at his home in Kent had arrived not long after she had left, and he had ridden there straightaway, not wanting his father's favorite home to be damaged permanently.

It had grown so late that he had considered staying the night, but the idea of sleeping so far away from his wife—especially when he did not know where she was going and who she was meeting—made him feel uneasy. And so he had risked footpads and highwaymen and ridden back in the dead of night.

He slept in a little later than usual, but when he entered the dining room, Anastasia was still there, even though her plate and cup were empty.

"Good morning," he said, nodding his head in greeting and taking his seat.

Her face pulled into a frown. "Is that all you've got to say?" There was clearly anger in her voice, though he wasn't really sure why.

"I do not think it is late enough that I need say 'good afternoon,' is it?" Laurence asked with a raised eyebrow. He was convinced he was the one being lied to, so he certainly did not feel like he deserved her anger.

"No one knew where you were! And you did not come back until long after everyone was in bed. I was—" She bit her bottom lip and looked down at the floor.

"You were what?"

"I was worried, of course," she snapped, her eyes meeting his in a blaze of fury. "Where were you? I came home and you were gone."

"Ah yes, while you were gone 'visiting your brother'," he said, irritation rising within him. They might be married, but that didn't give her any right to know his every movement—especially when he did not think she was being entirely honest with him.

"I did see my brother," she said, her cheeks flushing red. "Who did *you* see?"

There was an accusation there, he was sure, but he wasn't sure what she thought he was doing. He had not intended to hide his visit from her—she simply had not been there. Perhaps he should have left a note or told one of the staff...but he was used to being alone, without having to answer to anyone's concerns.

"There was an issue at one of my estates. I had to ride there to oversee the repairs."

Anastasia hesitated, as though she did not quite believe him, but she didn't say any more. Had the anger within her died down? He had never seen her so incensed. Normally she was so quiet, so diplomatic. Perhaps what they said about redheads was true: their tempers were fiery when provoked.

"I'm sorry if I worried you," he said, feeling a little guilty if she had been up worrying about him. It was rather nice to know that somebody cared, even if he wasn't used to having to share his movements.

She did not reply, and so Laurence sipped the coffee that the footman had brought in and tried to make conversation. "Do you have any plans for today?"

She folded her arms and glared out of the window. So it seemed her ire had not entirely cooled.

"I had thought… Never mind."

"What had you thought?"

Anastasia sighed. He watched her for a moment as she clearly decided whether or not to tell him what she had planned. Her red hair was pinned neatly, but in his mind's eye, he always saw it loose, her head thrown back in the throes of passion. Sometimes she seemed like two separate people, this wife of his—the quiet, meek woman in the day (well, other than today), and the enthusiastic, passionate woman who shared a bed with him every night.

Which was the real her?

She stuck her tongue between her teeth, bit it, and then continued. "I had thought that we might go on a picnic."

# CHAPTER TWENTY-ONE

THE SUN SHONE brightly in the perfectly blue sky, and they shaded themselves from it under a large oak tree in the park. Mrs. Turner, the cook, had sent a red-checked blanket along with their picnic, and as they sat there, the grass springy beneath the fabric, Laurence felt like a young lad again.

He couldn't remember the last time he'd had a picnic. He thought he remembered his nanny taking him when they were out on the Kent estate.

But that was a very long time ago indeed.

"What was it like, growing up with a brother?" Laurence asked as he peeled segments of an orange and popped them into his mouth. He offered one to Anastasia, and she took it with a smile.

She bit into the fruit before answering, and as droplets of juice ran down her chin, he had to fight the urge to lean forward and catch it on his tongue. Perhaps if they had been eating this fruit at home, he might have done so. But he couldn't—not in public. It wouldn't be right.

And what if it offended her?

"I always wanted a brother," Laurence confided as she finished the piece of fruit. "Or a sister, I suppose—but it was always a brother I imagined. A playmate, you know?"

Anastasia nodded. "I can understand wishing for one...but growing up with Oliver was not always pleasant."

Laurence was not wholly surprised by this revelation. Oliver did not seem like a particularly nice man, and so it was no stretch to think that he had not been a very kind boy.

"My father hated his brother. Even more so as they became adults, and my uncle frittered everything away. He even made me promise—" Laurence cut himself off, deciding in the moment that it might not be the most sensible thing to share. He didn't want her to think that he had aimed to trap her into marriage that night, on the dark walk. Although he had planned to find a wife, he certainly hadn't thought it would be like that. He wasn't entirely sure that she was happy in this marriage, and he didn't want to give her a reason to dislike him.

"He made you promise what?" Anastasia prompted, reaching for a slice of bread and some cheese. The picnic was even more delicious for its simplicity.

Laurence shook his head. "I can't remember what I was going to say. But you would not recommend growing up with a brother?"

"I cannot speak for all brothers," Anastasia began slowly. "But Oliver...well, I do not think he has ever liked me."

"I'm sure that can't be true," Laurence said with a frown.

She smiled sadly. "It is a realization I have only recently accepted, but I do not think he ever has. He would get very frustrated, as a child, and he would take it out on me."

"He would shout at you?" Laurence asked, picturing a little redheaded girl and a redheaded boy shouting at one another over the placement of a toy or who got the last sweet treat.

"Shout at me, hit me, lock me in the cupboard..." Anastasia spoke as if these things were normal, of little consequence—and yet they did not sound like the normal behaviors of a brother toward his younger sister.

"Did your parents never reprimand him? Or your nanny?"

Anastasia smiled ruefully. "Oliver has always been very good at knowing when he is not being watched—when he can get away with such behavior."

Laurence felt his hands curl into fists, as anger rose in his chest. "All this was only as children, though, yes?"

"It continued into our teenage years. Things got better when he left for university."

Laurence swallowed. While he did not like the thought of Anastasia being terrorized by her unpleasant older brother, at least it was no longer happening. "But he has not touched you in adulthood, has he?"

He did not miss the way her eyes darted away from his before she answered, all too breezily: "No, no, of course not."

His wife was a terrible liar. It was always clear when she was about to tell a falsehood, and he knew yet again that this was not the truth. He would not push it now—not ruin their picnic, their moment of connection. But if Oliver Carrington ever dared to lay a hand on his wife again, then he would rue the day.

ANASTASIA DID NOT like speaking of Oliver, or their difficult relationship. She had truly believed that the issues between them were in the past—until all this marriage business came up, until he had grabbed her wrist in the parlor that day. Now she felt the same fear that she had felt when she was a little girl.

But she didn't want to feel it today.

"What's it like to grow up knowing you're going to be a viscount one day?" she asked.

Laurence finished chewing the shortbread he had chosen from the selection of biscuits and cakes before answering. "When I was younger, I didn't really think about it. I mean, I was raised to know it would be my title one day, but my father didn't want it to be all I ever thought about. And then when I got older... Well, I realized that I would have this great power, this great responsibility—but that I would only get it once my father was dead." He gave a sad smile and pushed the plate of biscuits toward her.

"Unlike many of the ton, I liked my father. Loved him. And so I suppose the title has always been tinged with sadness, for me."

She could hear the anguish in his tone. She reached out and took his hand without thinking. He laced his fingers between hers.

"That was probably more detail than you wanted in answer to your question."

Anastasia shook her head and squeezed his hand tightly. "Not at all. I want… I want to get to know you. Properly."

# CHAPTER TWENTY-TWO

LAURENCE WAS RATHER surprised to find his heart beginning to race at the feel of her delicate fingers against his rough, calloused palms.

They had spent night after night making love, losing themselves in the ecstasy they found in each other's bodies. So why was such a simple touching of hands so intimate?

Their eyes met, and he leaned forward and pressed a kiss to the side of her lips, where the juice from the orange had run moments earlier.

She sighed quietly, and then moved her lips so that they pressed directly against his, and her tongue sought entry to his mouth. He could taste the orange she had been eating, and surely she could taste the same.

His fingertips moved to the nape of her neck, toying with a loose red curl there, trying to remember they were outdoors, and that anyone could see them, and that he shouldn't pull out every pin in her hair and lay her down in the grass and make her cry out his name.

Her fingertips anchored themselves in his hair, and she seemed to be having an equal amount of trouble remembering where they were. She pulled at his hair, drawing him tighter, lengthening the kiss until he could barely breathe.

And then she pulled away. Their eyes met, their chests both heaving, his lips presumably both as red and swollen as hers were.

Why had she stopped? For a moment, he wondered if she was still angry with him for being gone the previous night. He supposed he couldn't really blame her if she were. He knew if she had been gone and he hadn't known where she was, he would have been terrified, and angry, and not known what to do with himself.

But he didn't think it was anger burning in her eyes, but lust—a lust surely reflected in his own.

So why did she stop? Because they were outside? Because it was the middle of the day? He was about to open his mouth and just ask her, when she spoke, her voice breathy, the words staccato.

"I already know you like that," she said, her cheeks flushing a charming shade of pink. "We know…we know that part works."

He couldn't help but smirk. It certainly did work. That "part", as she called it—the sexual chemistry between them—was like nothing he had ever experienced, or even imagined possible. And he wanted to tell her that, but then he thought it might be rather callous to compare her out loud to other women he had been with—even if the comparison was such a positive.

"So you're saying…"

She bit her bottom lip. Did she know that only made him want to kiss her more? To take her into the stone pavilion, to make her forget that she had ever been angry with him, to make her forget even her own name…

"I'm saying that I want to get to know you. Properly."

"So no kissing," Laurence said with a sigh.

She tilted her head to one side. "Well, perhaps not *no* kissing…but we mustn't let it detract from the task at hand."

He nodded solemnly. "Your wish is my command. Just one more kiss then, and I promise I'll focus…"

THEY RETURNED HOME that evening, having stayed out picnicking until the sun began to set, and Anastasia was amazed at how light her heart felt compared with the night before. Did it truly matter where he had been the previous night, if he came home to her, and if he was so wonderful, so loving, so attentive…?

She told herself she couldn't let it matter. What they had was more important.

After supper, Laurence retired to his study, after wishing her a good night. She had said she wanted to go to bed early, after having so little sleep the night before, and so she left him and let the maid brush out her hair and help her into a nightgown. Her blasted bleeding had not stopped, and so there was no reason for Laurence to come to her room. She missed him being there. She missed their relations—but more than that, she missed his mere presence. Waking up in his arms, kissing him in the middle of the night…

He had said that when her bleeding no longer came, it would mean she was with child. And then he would stay with her always—would he not? Or perhaps she would be indisposed then too, and there would be no reason for him to join her…

She sat up in bed, envisioning months of him staying away, of the other women he might take to his bed, of how difficult it was to feel like she had no say in where he went, where he slept, whether he stayed the night.

And so, even though she had been exhausted from the previous night, once again she did not sleep. She heard Laurence come to bed, heard the soft conversation between him and his valet, heard the door close and him be left alone.

And that was when she decided. She did not have to have no say. After all, he had always left in the middle of the night—until she asked him not to.

Why couldn't this be the same?

Before she had a chance to change her mind, she strode across the bedroom and knocked on the door that joined the two rooms.

"Come in," he said in his deep voice.

She pushed the door open, and her breath was taken away by the sight of him sitting up in bed, shirtless, the muscles in his chest catching the light from a candle which flickered beside him.

He was breathtaking.

He beamed at her, his delight at seeing her clearly genuine, and held out his hand. "Are you well? I thought you would be asleep by now. I hope I didn't wake you..."

She shook her head. "You didn't wake me. I couldn't sleep. I..." She bit her bottom lip, trying to find the words, as he watched her expectantly, his hand still outstretched, lying on the bed, palm facing upwards.

She stepped toward him and reached out, taking his hand, thinking she might derive strength from being near him. In fact, the mere touch of his skin against hers made it even harder for her to think, and she had to force herself to focus through the haze of desire that always overwhelmed her when he was near.

"I was thinking..." she heard herself say, as though hearing someone else speak. "I was thinking that it is rather lonely on my own all night. That if we are to be parted every time I bleed, and perhaps when I am with child, then we would be separated an awful lot."

He squeezed her hand. "That is true."

"And I thought, if you are not too horrified or disgusted by the prospect, that perhaps you could sleep as you normally do in my bedchamber, and then when I am able to resume our... our...activities, you will know, and—" She rushed the words out in order to make herself finish saying them before embarrassment took hold, but he interrupted her.

"I miss you too, Anastasia. And I'm certainly not disgusted or horrified. I simply did not wish for you to feel like I was invading your space when you did not want me there."

"I want you there."

He threw back the covers, revealing that he wore nothing to bed when he slept alone either, making her blush. He did not let go of her hand, and she followed him back into her bedchamber, and settled into his arms, drifting off into a deep and restful sleep almost immediately.

# CHAPTER TWENTY-THREE

I T HAD BEEN an amazing week.

The best, she thought, since they had wed. She felt like she was finally getting to know who Laurence really was, and she liked him. She liked him a lot.

It was rather gratifying to know that they shared a connection that went beyond the physical. Not that she didn't appreciate that, of course. But it was a relief to know it wasn't all they had.

She wished she could tell him about the necklace she had pawned, but Oliver had made it clear that Laurence wasn't to know about his financial problems. And besides, Laurence would possibly be angry with her for taking it, for lying about where she was going—and she didn't want to ruin everything. Not when it was all going so well.

A week after their picnic, when her bleeding had stopped, they spent the night wrapped in one another's arms, and both rose late the next morning. After a leisurely breakfast and a kiss that was altogether too passionate for the dining room in the middle of the day, Laurence left to attend to some business, and Anastasia took tea in the parlor, feeling happy but a little tired. She hoped that when Laurence returned, they might go for a walk, or play cards, or just sit and talk. So for now she would rest, watch the people passing by the window, and drink tea.

A knock on the door interrupted that plan, and when the footman came in, carrying a silver tray with a calling card on it, her heart dropped. No one had paid her a visit here except for Oliver. She had been rather unknown before, and with a slightly scandalous marriage to the rakish viscount, no one in high society seemed to have been keen to seek her out. Not that she minded; she was happy enough with Laurence's company. In fact, she would have been happier if they were in the country, away from the noise and bustle of London—but that was a topic for another day.

She hoped it was not Oliver coming to see her, for he would surely spoil her good mood—and Laurence's too, if he came home and found him here. She did not think the two would ever be friends, and she couldn't blame Laurence. Her brother was not a very easy man.

"Mr. Carrington here to see you, Lady Walsham," the footman said with a bow of his head, and she felt her smile falter.

"Thank you. Please show him in."

She steeled herself for his entrance, and when he came in with a broad smile on his face, she felt panic rise in her chest.

He wanted something—she was sure.

"My darling sister," he said, embracing her.

Oh yes, he definitely wanted something.

"How are you, Oliver?"

"As well as can be expected," he said, and she did not know what that meant—and did not wish to ask him to find out.

"And you? You look well."

"I am, thank you."

She knew she ought to offer him tea, but she did not wish to prolong his visit. She had been feeling so happy; she didn't want all that joy to fall away.

There was an awkward silence for a moment or two, and then he clearly decided he didn't have time for small talk.

"The thing is, I'm afraid I need you to give me some more money."

She closed her eyes and said, "Not again, Oliver. We agreed."

"Yes, yes, I know. Very unfortunate. But you see, Baron Brett is still very frustrated about the way things turned out between you and him—"

"There was no me and him," Anastasia said hotly. "There was a marriage you arranged and I knew nothing about."

He waved his hand in the air as though her concerns were of no import. "Well, he decided that I owed interest on the money that I owed him, so what I paid was not enough. We must get this matter sorted, Anastasia. And you don't want Lord Walsham knowing about the Carrington financial affairs, do you? Or that you gave me money without telling him."

He gave a cold smile. So, he was going to blackmail her with the very deed she had committed to help him. Of course he was. She should have known. He couldn't be trusted—that had always been the case.

"I don't care if he knows about Carrington family finances," she said truthfully. "And perhaps him knowing that I gave you money is better than you endlessly asking me for it. Did you think of that, Oliver?"

"Who said anything about endlessly?" Oliver said. "Just once more, and then this whole matter can be put to rest. And Lord Walsham need never know about this distasteful business."

"I don't trust you, Oliver, when you say this will be the last time."

He gave her a hard stare. "And I don't think your husband would trust you, if he found out you'd been lying to him—stealing the family jewels. Do you want to risk him finding out?"

Anastasia swallowed. Perhaps it would be the last time. And then she wouldn't have to ruin everything with Laurence by admitting all this.

"How much do you need?"

Oliver's smile was back. The way his mood changed made her feel like she was a Catherine wheel, spinning out of control. "Two thousand pounds. So that we're done, once and for all."

She gasped. "So much more, Oliver—I don't know if I can... Are you sure Baron Brett isn't taking you for a fool, asking for that much more? On a debt of five hundred?"

Oliver took a step toward her and tipped her head up roughly to look him directly in the eyes. Her neck was bent at an awkward angle, and she could see the fury in his own eyes as he said, "Never call me a fool, Annie. Two thousand pounds is what I need, and it's what you're going to get me."

# CHAPTER TWENTY-FOUR

THE OWNER OF the pawnshop, a portly man in his late fifties, nodded his head in greeting to her, a look of recognition passing across his face.

She hated that he recognized who she was, and only hoped it was from her previous visit and not that he knew she was the Viscountess Walsham.

She didn't want word of this getting back to Laurence, nor did she want people thinking that he was hard up—that he had to send his wife to a pawnshop in order to fill his coffers.

"Good morning," she said, feeling sick to her stomach at even being here. *Again.* She had sworn last time there would be no repeat, and yet here she was, doing what Oliver had told her to. As always.

"Do you have another fine piece of jewelry for me, my lady?" he asked in a greasy voice.

*He's just assuming you have a title,* she told herself. *He can't know for sure.*

"What will you give me for this?" she asked, pulling the jeweled brooch out from her reticule. His greedy eyes lit up at the sight of it.

"Five hundred pounds," he said, reaching for it.

She pulled it back, out of his reach. "It is worth much more than that." In truth, she had no idea how much it was worth, but she had to assume he was trying to get away with offering less than its true value. And besides, what he was offering wasn't nearly enough to satisfy Oliver. And she did not wish to pawn anything else.

"I suppose I could stretch to eight hundred."

"One thousand," Anastasia insisted, trying to force her voice not to shake. She hated this whole interaction. But it was necessary. It still wouldn't be enough to get rid of Oliver, but at least she would be halfway.

He tilted his head from one side to the next, and then nodded. "Very well. You drive a hard bargain, Lady…"

She ignored the clear hint for her to give her name and handed the brooch over, finding it hard to let it go into his eager hands. "And the other piece I brought in is still here, yes?"

He nodded. "Yes, I'm a man of my word. You have four weeks from the date you brought it in to buy it back, before it goes on general sale."

Anastasia nodded. She had no idea how she would get the money together to buy it back in that time—especially with Oliver asking for more money, which would wipe out her pin money as well as what she had gotten for the pawned brooch. But she had to try. Maybe she could put all this right…

She wasn't sure she could convince herself that Oliver would not ask for money again. But she could be stronger. Say no this time. Stand up to him. She was an adult now. A married woman. She did not need to give in to her brother's every demand.

She shoved the money into her reticule and left the shop as quickly as she could, hoping never to have need to pawn anything again.

She was in such a hurry that she did not look where she was going as she exited, and she ran straight into a man on the other side of the door.

"Goodness me, I'm so sorry," she said, hastily picking up her reticule, which she had dropped, and straightening herself up.

Her blood turned cold in her veins as she saw the man into whom she had walked.

He gave her a leering smile, and then straightened his waist-coat. "No need to apologize, Lady Walsham. No harm done."

"I am pleased to hear that, Lord Brett," Anastasia said through gritted teeth.

"I must say, I'm surprised to see you at this end of town. Is the viscount happy with his wife being out, alone, in such a district?"

A wave of nausea threatened to overwhelm her. He was going to ruin it all. He was going to tell Laurence, and then her husband would hate her, and everything they'd been building would be ruined.

"I had not realized I had wandered so far downtown. Forgive me, Lord Brett, but I must be leaving." Perhaps she could tell Laurence where she had been before Lord Brett had a chance to. She could think of an excuse and make everything all right.

But as she turned to walk away, Lord Brett reached out and grabbed her wrist. "Not so fast, Lady Walsham. It is rather fortuitous that I've run into you here, for I believe your brother has been avoiding me."

Anastasia swallowed and looked around for someone to help her—but no one looked in her direction. They kept their eyes to the ground, clearly wanting to mind their own business.

"I no longer live with my brother, so I do not know—"

His grip on her wrist tightened, and she sucked in her breath, wondering whether he would leave a bruise.

"Your brother owes me."

Anastasia nodded. She did not know what else to do.

"He was going to pay me with a virgin bride—but as you know, that did not go to plan."

Anastasia was afraid that if she opened her mouth she would throw up, and so she kept silent, hoping he merely meant her to pass some message on to Oliver, and would soon let her go.

"And now he has not stuck to his word. I am a fair man, so I do not expect to be treated like this. You will tell him—I will have what I'm owed by the end of the month."

Anastasia nodded, desperate to get away from him.

"And if I do not…well, I will take what is owed. In any form I can."

He gave her a look that made fear and dread fill her soul. And then he let go.

For a moment she stood there, too stunned to move. And then she half-walked, half-ran to the street where she had left her maid and the carriage.

# CHAPTER TWENTY-FIVE

"THIS IS THE last time, Oliver," Anastasia said—and not for the first time.

"Of course it is. Just get the rest of the two thousand pounds, and then this is over."

She doubted he even believed that himself.

"I mean it, Oliver. I don't like lying to Laurence. It's not right, keeping secrets from my husband."

"You think he doesn't keep secrets from you?" Oliver scoffed.

"I—this—no—that is…"

"Come on, you're not stupid. You know the man's reputation. Hell, you know the reason the two of you ended up married."

Anastasia frowned. She tried not to think of her husband's reputation—not because she thought it mattered what he had done before they were married, but because she couldn't help but wonder if he still continued in such a way now. Whenever he disappeared, that was where her mind went.

She also knew that nothing truly improper had happened between her and Laurence before they had said their vows. He had been kind and even honorable when faced with her potential ruination.

He was a good man. She was sure of that.

What she wasn't entirely sure of was whether he could curb the side of himself that had garnered such a reputation—or whether he even thought he ought to.

"Ask him about Lady Frindley if you want to know whether he has any secrets. Or Mrs. Askew. Or—"

"Enough!" It was all Anastasia could do not to put a hand over her ears. She did not want to hear these words—whether or not they were true, or just Oliver trying to hurt her. She did not need to give her imagination any more ammunition.

And she also knew she would never be bold enough to ask Laurence outright about these women.

Because what if it turned out to be true? How would she go on if she knew for certain that she was not her husband's only lover? She did not know if she could continue to smile and be happy if that was confirmed. Because she felt something deeper for Laurence than she had ever expected to—something that she thought might possibly be approaching love, although of course, she had no other experience to compare it to.

A catlike smile spread across Oliver's face, and she knew he could tell he'd needled her.

"Not to worry, dear sister. This will ever remain between us, and your husband's business will remain private, and everyone can go on as if nothing is amiss."

HE FOLLOWED HER at a discreet distance, feeling more and more puzzled as they made their way further downtown, to an area of London where no gently bred lady would be expected to shop— or even visit. What on earth was she doing here? Had she taken a lowborn lover?

The carriage stopped abruptly, and Laurence pulled the reins of his mount, wanting to make sure he stayed out of sight. He walked the horse over to a side street where he could see the carriage but did not think the occupant would be able to see him.

Anastasia did indeed get out, looking furtively around her as she did so. He stayed back and held his breath, but no one else exited the coach.

She did not enter any of the ramshackle houses on the street but set off at a purposeful pace down the road. When she turned the corner, out of sight, he followed on, his heart pounding in his chest.

He rounded the corner just in time to see her entering the shop, although he could not read the name on the lintel from this distance.

He took heart from the fact that she was not in there long—and certainly not long enough to be visiting a lover.

With a start, he realized that she was returning in his direction, and he urged his horse down an alleyway where he hoped she would not look.

He watched her pass, though, looking as beautiful as ever. Her face was set in a determined grimace, and she held on tightly to her reticule, as though afraid it might be stolen from her.

In this neck of the woods, she might not be far wrong. Laurence wanted to jump out and protect her, to tell her how foolish it was to wander these streets at all, let alone unchaperoned.

He could not alert her to his presence. He needed to know where she was going. He needed to protect her—because he was her husband. That was what he was meant to do. And it was what he wanted to do, too.

Once she was back in the carriage, he urged his horse into a trot and stopped outside the mysterious shop.

*Smith & Sons Pawnbrokers. Established 1763.*

A pawnbroker? It made no sense. He gave her a generous allowance and had told her to put anything she liked onto his accounts. And if she needed money, she had only to ask—he was more than happy to share. So why was she visiting a pawnbroker?

And what did she have to pawn? While not poor, the Carringtons certainly had not been well-off, and her dastardly brother had sold anything of value in order to fund his gambling habits. So he thought it unlikely she had come to the marriage with any jewels hidden away.

The situation seemed even more mysterious than it had been before he had followed her, and he considered going into the shop and questioning the proprietor. But the man would surely tell Anastasia if she returned…and he did not want her to know he had been following her.

He just wanted to know what she was doing—and why she felt the need to keep it from him.

# CHAPTER TWENTY-SIX

THAT EVENING, LAURENCE felt the need for a little space, to mull over what he had seen, without losing himself in Anastasia's embrace. He considered going to the club, but he found himself entering the nearby gambling hell instead. He was not one to fritter money away—never had been—but he thought he could be distracted from his concerns for an hour too.

He was not surprised to see Oliver Carrington in the gambling hell, nor Lord Brett. He found both men rather distasteful, but he had no issue with men choosing to gamble if they so wished—as long as they had the money to do so. He thought it rather a pointless pastime himself, but he had no desire to judge the choices of others.

He rather thought his choice of venue for the evening had been a little silly, since he had no wish to gamble—but he ordered a drink and watched as others won and lost fortunes on a roll of the dice.

As his gaze wandered over the large room, he was struck with a sense of recognition of one of the men at the poker table.

Not wanting to look like he was staring, he continued looking around before returning his eyes to the man in question, trying to figure out where he knew him from. He was an older man, with a trimmed goatee and a balding head. He certainly was not someone that Laurence had been to school with, nor someone who frequented the same social circles. In fact, the man looked more of an age with Laurence's father.

And then it struck him.

The man was surely his Uncle Thomas, his father's younger brother—the man who was so reckless that his father had always been insistent he must never be allowed to inherit.

Laurence had not seen him since that night in Vauxhall Gardens, when his father had extracted the promise from him that he must wed and sire an heir. His uncle had aged since then, and the facial hair made him look like an entirely different man.

Perhaps that was the point.

He had surely been staring too long, and the attention had been felt, for the man looked up, caught his eye, and then smirked.

As he stood up from the table, Laurence wondered whether he ought to leave, but it was too late. He already had him in his sights. And besides, why shouldn't he speak to the man? Just because he had never got on with his father didn't mean Laurence could not pass the time of day with him.

"Why, if it isn't little Larry," his uncle said in a rather derisive tone. "Or should I say Lord Walsham." He gave a mock bow, and Laurence told himself to rise above it. There was no point arguing with the man here.

"Good evening, Uncle Thomas. It has been a long time."

"It has indeed," Thomas said. "I was sorry to hear about my brother's passing." His tone suggested he felt anything but sorry, and Laurence rather thought that if he had felt even the slightest bereaved, he would have attended the funeral.

But there was no point in raising that now. It would make no difference. And talking of his father—and his funeral—only made Laurence morose.

"Thank you," he said simply.

"And I hear you have been recently wed?"

"Indeed."

"My congratulations," Thomas said, though there was irritation behind his eyes. "Of course, I am sure you are aware that until you have a son, I am the heir to the title of Viscount Walsham."

This made Laurence grit his teeth. "I understand the genealogy, yes."

"I'm sure you are doing your duty diligently, ensuring there are plenty of Walsham heirs to fill that fine estate," Thomas said, a lascivious grin upon his lips. "But just remember—I'm next in line. Your father was always so pleased about that fact."

Laurence knew that his uncle was well aware that that was a falsehood, just as he knew that Thomas was simply trying to get a reaction from him. He wasn't sure why; perhaps just for the sake of it. But he was determined not to give him what he desired.

"Well, it has been a pleasure to see you again, uncle," Laurence lied. "I will bid you good evening, for I have business to attend to."

He felt the man's eyes upon him as he walked out of the gambling hell, choosing to pass the evening in his club instead. He was a strange man, his uncle—and still apparently keen on gambling away his fortune. Whatever was left of it, anyway.

Laurence would feel altogether happier once he had a son: his promise to his father would be fulfilled, and his uncle pushed even further down the list of heirs to the title.

AFTER SHE HAD given Oliver the rest of the two thousand pounds, Anastasia thought it was at an end. For the next six weeks, she did not see her brother, and as the Season wound down, she and Laurence spent more time together, uninterrupted.

She thought that perhaps she would suggest going to his estate in Kent, when everyone had left the city. Maybe then he would wish to return to the country.

But then that calling card appeared on a silver tray once more, and her hopes were dashed.

"No, Oliver," she said, as she had done many times before. "I'm done. You keep saying you've paid everything off, and then you're right back where you started. I cannot keep—"

Oliver reached out and grabbed her upper arm, his fingers biting into the flesh.

"When are you going to learn to do as you're told?"

At this, Anastasia choked back a sob. His eyes were ablaze, and his grip was only getting tighter.

"If you had married Baron Brett, none of this would be a problem. But instead, you acted like a common whore, and now I must make everything right."

Anastasia shook her head, tears falling down her face.

"I did not, and I will not help you anymore."

Not only had she not done anything improper with Laurence before they were wed, she also did not believe that had she married Baron Brett, all would be well. Perhaps it would have paid off Oliver's debts to that man, but it seemed there was an endless number of odious men ready to come out of the woodwork and insist he pay debts he had racked up. Not to mention that he just seemed very capable of amassing new ones.

He shook her—once, twice—hard enough to make her head wobble.

"Don't be a fool, Anastasia, as you have been your entire life."

And whether it was the realization she'd had that morning—that it had been the longest she had ever not bled for, and that therefore there was a chance that she had a life to protect other than her own—or whether she had just finally had enough, she did not know.

But her hand flew to his, and she tried to pry it off as she said, for the final time:

"No. Take your hand off me, or I will scream, and the staff will come running, and everyone will know what you are."

She could tell by the look in his eyes that he did not believe her. His grip tightened further, and she opened her mouth, ready to follow through on her threat—when the door opened before she had the chance.

"If you want to keep that hand, I suggest you take it off my wife immediately."

*Laurence.*

Her heart soared, even though his tone was steely and his eyes full of anger—and there was a good chance that his arrival in the middle of this horrible scene would mean she had to tell him what had been going on.

But he was here. And he wouldn't let Oliver harm her. She'd known in her heart that he would always keep her safe.

It was one of the things she loved about him.

Oliver laughed and let go of her arm. She rubbed it as the blood flow returned, hoping to erase the imprint of his fingers upon her skin.

"No need to take everything so seriously, Laurence," Oliver said, turning his back on Anastasia. "Merely a little disagreement between siblings—nothing for you to get involved in. I'm sure you know by now that Anastasia can be rather a handful. Sometimes she needs to be reminded of who is in charge."

Anger roared up inside Anastasia, but it was nothing compared to the fury she saw in her husband's eyes. He took a step toward Oliver, and she was sure they were going to come to blows.

"You may call me 'Lord Walsham'," was all Laurence said, his voice surprisingly steady—although Anastasia could see his hands, which had balled into fists, shaking slightly.

"And I must remind you: you have no legal charge over my wife. If you touch her again, I will kill you."

Oliver laughed again, but it was hollow this time. He might not have believed Anastasia's threats, but he certainly seemed to believe Laurence's.

"Lord Walsham, I—"

"You are not welcome in this house. Leave now—and if you ever touch my wife again, you will need to name your second, and I will meet you at Hyde Park. And I warn you, I am a very good shot."

Oliver paled and stalked from the room without another word.

Anastasia breathed a sigh of relief, and then felt her legs buckling as the stress of the day threatened to overwhelm her. Laurence rushed forward, his hand around her waist before she could crumple to the ground. She leaned her head against his solid form, breathed in the woody scent she would always associate with him, and felt her heart rate slow back to its normal rhythm.

This was where she belonged. This was where she was safe—in Laurence's arms.

"Did he hurt you?" Laurence asked.

Anastasia shook her head. Well, he hadn't seriously hurt her, anyway. Whether he would have done so if Laurence had not entered the room, she could not say.

"I thought you wouldn't be home until tonight."

"I didn't plan to be. But I…"

She looked up into his eyes, and her heart skipped a beat.

"I missed you."

Her face broke into a smile, even in spite of the misery of the situation.

"You did?"

He nodded solemnly.

"I did. Although perhaps you wished I'd stayed away—not come in and threatened your brother. Although he's lucky all I did was threaten him."

She shook her head and then buried it in his shoulder.

"I'm glad you're home," she said in a whisper.

"Are you going to tell me what that was all about?" he asked.

Anastasia bit her lip.

"I—" It was so hard to find the words. "I will," she promised. "But…could it not be today?"

# CHAPTER TWENTY-SEVEN

HE MANEUVERED THEM both to the sofa in the center of the room and sat down, holding her close. He didn't want her to explain it another day—he wanted her to tell him *now*.

Well, what he really wanted to do was hunt down Oliver Carrington and make him pay for hurting his wife.

But she had not trusted him enough to tell him whatever was going on, and so he would not push her. Not today. He wanted her to know that she could trust him—that he only wanted what was best for her. And if she came to that realization on her own, then it would surely be better.

He presumed whatever was going on with Oliver was linked to the pawnshop he had seen her going to. And he wanted to tell her not to worry, to ask if she needed money, to suggest that they just leave London and all of this behind them and disappear into the countryside.

And perhaps he would—but not today. Today, he needed to be there for her.

She leaned her head against his chest, and he stroked her hair absentmindedly, knocking free some of the pins. She didn't seem to mind. Instead, her body relaxed in his arms, and when he looked down, her eyes had fluttered closed, although her breathing suggested she was still awake.

"Sometimes I think I might have been better off not having a brother, however much I wished for one," Laurence said.

Anastasia gave a short, sharp laugh. "You might be right."

"Although I hope, when we have children, they will not have such issues with their siblings. Not like you and Oliver, or my father and his brother."

She seemed to stiffen in his arms again at the mention of children. He hoped she didn't think he was pressuring her; after all, these things took time. It wasn't as though they weren't doing everything they could to try to conceive. He was sure it would happen, eventually.

"You never told me... What went wrong between your father and his brother?"

"I don't know all the details. I've only met him a handful of times, because the feud goes back many years."

"Oh, so he's still alive then?" Anastasia said, sounding surprised.

Laurence nodded and continued to card his fingers through her hair.

"Yes—he's quite a bit younger than my father. All I really knew was that he had wasted a lot of money, gambled it away, brought disrepute on the family name. It was why my father was so insistent that he should never be able to inherit the title or the estates."

He had shared his thoughts without thinking, but he wished he had not when she pulled her head back and looked up into his eyes.

"How could he ensure that, if his brother had a right to inherit?"

Laurence licked his lips, which had suddenly gone dry, and tried to decide whether she would be offended at the notion that he had married her because he needed to marry and reproduce. But then, she surely knew it was not a love match. The circumstances had certainly not been that way for either of them.

"He made me promise on his deathbed that I would settle down, marry, and produce an heir. So that his brother would be less likely to ever inherit."

He pressed a kiss to her forehead and grinned. "And I'm sure you can agree that we are certainly doing our best on that score."

ANASTASIA BLUSHED AT the suggestive nature of his words and tried to smile, but found she could not. Whilst his words were true, they prickled uncomfortably in her heart.

The fact that he had promised his father he would wed and produce an heir did not concern her. After all, whether or not it had been promised, that was the aim of most gentlemen who married—and she had known from the beginning that she would be expected to carry the future Lord Walsham.

The fact that she might be carrying him at this very moment both excited and terrified her.

No, that wasn't what made her uncomfortable. It was the thought that all those nights on which they had made love—the nights where she'd felt they had truly had a connection, the nights which had given her hope for a successful marriage... It seemed they had only been in pursuit of conceiving a child. And that had only been because of a promise he made to his beloved father.

None of it was for Anastasia, or inspired by her. It was all duty...and she had been foolish to think otherwise.

She had hoped for something more than an arranged marriage—and she had thought, perhaps, that they had been building toward it. Not just with the pleasure they shared at night, but also with the time they had begun to spend with one another in the day, the questions they had asked, the knowledge they had shared.

But now it seemed she had been kidding herself, giving in to foolish romantic notions. And who had she hurt, save for herself?

He had a reputation among women, as her brother had so gleefully reminded her. And those names he had taunted her with stuck in her mind: *Lady Frindley. Mrs. Askew.*

"Are you well?" Laurence asked. "You look rather pale."

She swallowed back ridiculous tears and nodded.

"Yes, thank you. I just think this whole ordeal has exhausted me. I think I must be alone, to lie down for a while."

He nodded, standing as she did, and followed her to the door.

"Of course. If you need anything, I'm happy to—"

"I'll be fine, thank you. You've done plenty today."

She hurried from the room before the tears could fall, for she had no idea how she would explain her emotions to him. What would she tell him? *I think I'm in love with you? I thought you loved me? I've only just realized I'm merely a broodmare?*

*No.* It was better to keep all of that locked away, and to keep her distance until she was confident she could keep a lid on her emotions.

As she lay on her bed, staring up at the blue canopy above it, she rested a hand on her stomach. It had been weeks and weeks since she had bled. She had not paid an awful lot of attention to such things in the past, but she was fairly sure that this was the longest she had ever gone since her courses had started. Was it just a coincidence? Or had they indeed conceived the child that Laurence—and his father—so wished for?

She imagined that she was growing such a life inside her—and in her mind's eye, it was a little boy who looked just like Laurence. It wasn't only him who wished for a child. Being a mother would surely be a wonderful experience. Somebody to love, somebody who would always love her.

Even if Laurence didn't.

# CHAPTER TWENTY-EIGHT

LAURENCE DID NOT like being alone in the ballroom. He was only attending because he'd thought Anastasia might enjoy it. She had seemed rather low of late, especially since the incident with her brother, which she still did not wish to explain.

But just as they had been about to leave for the out-of-Season event hosted by Lord and Lady Jones, she'd had an attack of sickness, and yet insisted that he still attend alone.

That had certainly not been what he had wished for. Such events had been admittedly enjoyable enough when he had been flirting and dancing with every woman there, looking for the next lovely lady to warm his bed.

But such things held no interest for him now. He had realized, over the last few weeks, that there was only one lady he wanted in his bed.

And she was currently asleep and ill in her own.

Still, he pasted on a smile, greeted the hosts, and procured a glass of wine. He did not plan on staying long—just long enough that he would not appear rude. In truth, all he wanted to do was get back to Anastasia, to see how she was faring, to see if she needed anything.

He was a rather different man than he had been the last time he had frequented society ballrooms.

"Lord Walsham! We have not seen you nearly often enough of late." He turned around to see Lady Gillespie, a woman who had been widowed young and with whom Laurence had enjoyed a brief affair two years prior.

"Lady Gillespie," he said, bowing his head. "It is a pleasure to see you, as always."

"We have been denied your handsome face far too much since you wed, have we not, Caroline?" His heart dropped as she pulled her friend into the conversation. For Caroline was known to the world as Lady Frindley, and although Laurence's time with her had also been pleasant, its ending had been far more complicated.

She had wanted what he was not willing to give: commitment.

"Indeed, it is a great shame."

"And I have not even met your wife yet, although of course Caroline was at the wedding. A pretty little redhead, so I hear. With the two of you locked away in your London home all these weeks, the rumors are that it's a love match." She smiled at him wolfishly, clearly fishing for gossip.

"Who am I to argue with rumor?" Laurence said, keen to extricate himself from the conversation. "If you'll excuse me, ladies, I see a friend I must speak with."

"Of course," Lady Gillespie said. "But you must save a dance for each of us, Walsham."

Laurence nodded and smiled as he hurried away, with no intention of dancing with either woman. In fact, he did not intend to dance at all. What was the point, with Anastasia not there?

As he did not want them to see him failing to meet his fictitious friend, he hurried out into the hallway and across the hall to where many gentlemen were playing cards.

So, London now thought theirs was a love match. The gossips had surely known initially that it was not. The rumor mill had gone wild at the fact that the notorious Lord Walsham had been caught on the dark walk with an innocent young lady and had been forced to wed her.

But obviously, the time they were spending together—and

the lack of time they were spending elsewhere—had made people rethink the situation. Well, he would much rather that they were gossiping about it being a love match than about the situation in Vauxhall Gardens, even if it weren't true.

Because it wasn't true. He hadn't married her for love. What he felt for her now…

Was that love? Wanting to be with her, and not with anyone else? Wanting to protect her, no matter the cost? Wanting her to be happy, even if it meant her hiding things from him?

Those two women he had spent many enjoyable hours with had certainly given him a lot to think about.

He did not plan to play cards, but the room was quieter, and he was less likely to be cornered or pushed into dancing. His eyes flicked around the room and landed on a figure he did not wish to see, but he supposed he should not have been surprised to encounter: His brother-in-law, Oliver Carrington.

Carrington had spotted him too, and he waved his hand in greeting. Laurence did not wave back. He did not understand why his brother-in-law was making his presence known at all, considering what had happened the last time they had met. Did he think all was forgotten, or forgiven, because they were in a different setting?

Clearly, he did—because when he lowered his hand, he came over to where Laurence was standing, drinking his wine and watching.

"Good evening, Walsham." Well, at least he had not tried to use his Christian name again.

"Carrington." He had no wish to wish him a good evening.

"Enjoying a little freedom away from my sister?" he asked, with a nasty smile on his face.

The urge to punch him right in his obnoxious mouth filled Laurence's chest, and only the rules of common decency stopped him. But if Oliver pushed any further, that might not be enough.

"I suggest you walk away now, and do not speak of my wife like that again."

"Well, I must be going," Carrington said, as though Laurence had not been the one to dismiss him.

"The cards are in my favor tonight, I'm sure of it—I just need to find the right table…"

He did not wish to stay in the card room, watching Oliver throw away good money after bad, and so he turned and exited the room, intending to head back to the ballroom for a little while before making his excuses and going home.

But he found himself face-to-face with Lady Frindley, her fan coyly in front of her face, her eyes full of joy at the chance meeting.

Whether or not it was truly chance, Laurence wasn't sure.

"I'd hoped I might see you alone," Lady Frindley said, reaching out to trail a finger down the center of his cravat.

Once, such a move might have made him keen to find a dark corner, to whisk her away from prying eyes and have his way with her.

But today, it made him recoil. It was not her fault, particularly—she just wasn't the one he wanted to be in his personal space. And he thought he'd made his feelings clear when they had last met, in Russell Square.

"I was on my way home, Lady Frindley," he said, leaning back a little to put distance between them.

She gave a sly grin.

"No need to be so formal when it's just the two of us, Laurence."

But he felt every need to be formal. He wanted to put distance between the relationship they'd had before and the way things were now. He did not want her getting the wrong idea—or anyone else, for that matter. He was sure Anastasia would be hurt if she heard rumors that he had been close with Lady Frindley, even if she was unlikely to know of their former connection.

He knew how he would feel if he heard that she had been close to another man, at any rate—and he would not wish to inflict that upon her.

"Surely you're bored of that young wife of yours by now," Lady Frindley said, the smile not leaving her lips, "and ready to spend time once more with a woman who knows what she is doing." She wet her lips seductively with her tongue and gave him a knowing look. She never seemed to give up.

"Caroline, I—"

She leaned in, her lips hovering an inch away from his, and whispered,

"It would be our little secret."

It would have been so easy to close the gap, to kiss her and fall into bed with her like old times, to be the man that everyone already thought he was.

But the image of Anastasia in his mind was a powerful deterrent. He didn't want Caroline. He didn't want meaningless, emotionless sex. He wanted Anastasia. He wanted this marriage. He wanted love.

The emotion was so strong that he almost shoved Lady Frindley away from him—but thankfully, he realized what he was about to do and stopped himself. Whatever he was feeling, it certainly wasn't acceptable to push a woman.

"No, thank you," he said forcefully, striding toward the door that led to the cool night air, deciding that it was very definitely time to go home.

As he left, he caught sight of Oliver Carrington and Baron Brett, watching him closely. He was sure they had seen the interaction with Lady Frindley—but if they had, they must have seen that he had moved away from her, that he would not do anything to hurt Anastasia.

Not that he thought either of them particularly cared about whether they hurt Anastasia or not.

ANASTASIA WISHED THERE were someone she could speak to about

her suspicions that she was with child. The sickness she had certainly heard of as a symptom, but what of the rest? The sore breasts, the inability to sleep, the strange dreams… Were these signs too? And how would she know when she should expect the arrival? Did she need to consult with a doctor? It was all so unknown to her.

When her maid came in that morning, Anastasia presumed her anguish was apparent, for she paused in her brushing more than once to ask if her mistress was well.

The third time she asked, Anastasia cracked. The maid was not married, but she rather thought that she might know a little more of life than Anastasia did herself.

"Do you know, Kate, how one tells…if one is with child?" It was such a hard question to ask, and yet she immediately felt relief at having shared her burden with somebody—anybody.

The maid's face broke into a smile. "Well, my lady. There is the ceasing of your monthly bleed…"

Anastasia nodded. She knew about that one.

"And then the thickening around the middle, as the babe grows. I believe…that is, my sisters have told me that their breasts grow bigger too, as they prepare for milk."

"And can they hurt, too?" Anastasia asked, feeling bolder as she began to get answers.

"I believe so," Kate said with a nod.

"And how would you know…when the baby is to be born?"

"You must count, I believe, from your last bleed. Nine months."

Anastasia sighed.

"And if that bleeding is not always regular?"

Anastasia met her maid's glance in the mirror, and Kate gave a sad smile and a shrug.

"I am afraid I do not know, my lady. My knowledge is only from when my mother had younger brothers and sisters, and when my sisters had their own babes. Perhaps a doctor…"

Anastasia nodded, blushing even at the thought of sharing

such information with a male physician.

"Thank you. These questions…they are merely an interest, you see. I would not wish them to leave this room."

The maid ducked her head. "Of course not, my lady."

Once again, Anastasia was left in the dark. Who could she ask? If only she had more confidence in Laurence.

# CHAPTER TWENTY-NINE

ANASTASIA HAD BEEN asleep when he got home the previous night. He had still climbed into bed with her because it seemed that was what she wanted. And it was what he wanted, too. Since she had come to him and asked him to return to her bed, he had not left it. They might not have made love every night, but they had certainly slept together.

Yes, he supposed he could see why the ton thought it was a love match. They were certainly acting like a couple very much in love...

By the time he awoke, Anastasia had already gotten up for the day. She was sitting at the breakfast table with a piece of dry toast in front of her.

"How are you feeling?" he asked.

"Much better, thank you," she said, although he still thought she looked rather pale, and she clearly didn't have her usual appetite. Still, he was pleased to see her out of bed and ready to face the day.

"How was the ball?" she asked, and he chewed on his own piece of toast for a few moments to give himself time to think of a reply. He did not wish to mention Lady Frindley, nor seeing Oliver. But that didn't leave much to discuss...

"Fine," he said in the end, reaching for his coffee. "Dull, nothing new. I had no real wish to attend without you, as you know."

She smiled, but it did not quite reach her eyes. Their connection seemed as deep as ever—in the bedchamber at least—and yet he couldn't help but feel that sometimes her happiness was not altogether real. However, he didn't know what had happened to upset the balance.

Perhaps he was just imagining things.

"Was it well attended?" she asked. "With the Season dwindling, I thought it might be rather quiet."

There were certainly many in attendance that he wished had not been—Lady Frindley and Mrs. Askew among them.

"If I'm honest, I didn't stay very long. I was home well before midnight. But you were already fast asleep. Is that a new dress?" he asked, hoping to move the conversation in a different direction. He hadn't particularly thought he'd done anything wrong, but he found himself uncomfortable talking about the ball and thinking about his conversation with Lady Frindley.

"Oh," she said, seeming surprised at the change in topic. "Yes, it is. I hope you don't mind…"

She ran her hands down the dark green fabric of the day dress, and Laurence smiled. "Of course I don't mind. It looks very pretty on you."

She blushed, and her eyes fluttered downward. "Thank you."

"In fact, I think there's a necklace in the jewelry box upstairs that would go very well with it. Silver, with emeralds. I think it was my grandmother's—you should look it out."

Her face went even paler, and he worried that whatever had ailed her the night before had returned.

She nodded. "I'll—I'll have a look. Please, excuse me," she said, standing quickly and hurrying from the room.

He stood but let her go, getting the feeling that she wanted to be alone.

SHE RAN TO the chamber pot and threw up the few bites of toast she had managed to eat at breakfast.

The necklace. The blasted necklace. She had pawned it for the very first payment Oliver had requested.

She had thought he wouldn't notice that it was gone. That he wouldn't know what jewelry his mother or grandmother—or great-grandmother, for that matter—had possessed. She had checked that it wasn't an item of sentimental value…

And yet he remembered it. Described it exactly. And wanted to see her wear it.

But she couldn't. She hadn't been able to afford to buy it back from the pawnshop, and she didn't even know whether it would still be there. After all, the four-week period she'd had to buy it back before it went on general sale was long over.

She sat down on the stone floor and tried desperately to think of a plan. How could she get the money? Five hundred pounds… It wasn't a huge sum to Laurence, but she couldn't just ask him for it. She had a little pin money which she had managed to keep from Oliver, but that wasn't enough. She looked down at the new emerald dress. She could sell that, she supposed. And two or three of the other new gowns she owned. And maybe there was something else she could pawn, although that would surely land her in a similar situation again. She ran her hands over her face.

She had felt unhappiness pervading her mood since she had realized that Laurence only really wanted her in order to sire an heir. It had been hard to shake off, but now it was dread that took over. Dread that Laurence would find out she had pawned the jewelry. Dread that he would find out she had lied, that she had given the money to Oliver, that she hadn't come to him—when she so clearly ought to have done.

That she hadn't trusted him enough to let him handle it.

She had to get the necklace back. And so she tore through her room, finding anything she could possibly sell that Laurence would not notice, and hoped it would be enough.

# CHAPTER THIRTY

ANASTASIA HELD THE parcel tightly in one hand, feeling a sense of relief at having it back in her possession. It was only one of the pieces she'd sold, of course, but it was the one that Laurence had mentioned—and knowing she would not have to lie about its whereabouts lightened her heavy heart.

She hurried back to where she had left the carriage and her maid, wondering what the young woman thought of all these mysterious trips. Perhaps she thought that Anastasia was having an affair with another man—even though nothing could be further from the truth.

Anastasia wanted no one but Laurence. She only hoped that one day he might feel the same.

She didn't look around as she turned the corner, her mind on getting home, and whether Laurence would be there, and what they might talk about over supper.

When a hand reached out and pulled her roughly into an alleyway, it took her a moment to react—and by the time she had opened her mouth to scream, a wad of fabric had already been shoved into it, rendering her silent.

Panic tore through her body, making it hard to breathe, making it hard to think. She tried to get a look at who had seized her from the street, but she was marched roughly forward, her attacker remaining behind, hastening her movements with a hard shove between her shoulder blades whenever she slowed down.

She considered running, but he—and she knew it was a man, even without being able to see him, because of the size of the hand that gripped her, and the presence looming above her—had such a tight hold on her shoulder that she did not think she could get away. And if she could, where would she run? She had no idea what was at the end of this alley. Perhaps he had accomplices, henchmen. Was he a footpad, wanting to take her jewels? He could have them…

Except…she had worked so hard to get back the necklace. How heartbreaking it would be to see it taken by some thief. She supposed then she would have a legitimate reason to tell Laurence why she did not wear it. Although then she would have to lie about where it had been stolen, for there was no good reason she could give for being in this part of town.

She hated the web of lies she seemed to have ensnared herself in.

What if he wasn't merely a footpad? What if jewels alone would not make him leave? That was a thought too horrible to contemplate. She knew there were evil men in the world…she had always just hoped they would never want anything to do with her.

She tried to protest as she was bundled into a coach waiting at the end of the alleyway, but her muffled words only earned her a kick in the ankles.

The carriage was empty, but her attacker followed her inside, slamming the door, hitting his cane on the roof to tell the driver to go, and then sitting opposite her.

And then she saw his identity.

And her blood ran cold.

Instinctively, a hand flew to her stomach to protect the life that she was sure was growing inside—her baby, Laurence's baby. Because this was an evil man, and she did not think it was her jewels that he wanted.

He smiled slowly, and then put his hand upon her knee. It took everything in her not to kick him off, but she did not think that angering him was the right decision. She just needed to get away from him, as soon as possible. Surely Laurence would notice she was missing soon, would try to find her…

A voice in the back of her head told her that Laurence would not notice that she was gone until he sat down at supper and she was not there. And that moment was probably still hours away.

And a lot could happen in the space of hours.

"Now, if I remove the gag, do you promise not to scream?"

As much as it sickened her to do so, she nodded. She was struggling to breathe, with the panic and the cloth filling her mouth, and it would be a blessed relief for it to be removed.

He reached forward and pulled the fabric from her mouth.

"Lord Brett," Anastasia said after several tries, her mouth so dry it was hard to speak. "You must let me go at once."

Baron Brett laughed, and the sound rang in her ears and made her want to scream.

But she had promised not to.

"I certainly do not need to let you go. And, I'm afraid, I will not be."

Anastasia tried to remain calm and told herself that angering him would only make things worse.

"I do not understand. What—what do you want with me?"

He chuckled.

"I think you know exactly what I want with you," he said with a lascivious grin that made her want to vomit. "And you should have been mine. You were the payment that your brother owed—that he still owes. And I'm tired of waiting."

Anastasia shook her head, and when she spoke, her voice was higher than she had ever heard it before.

"No, no, my brother had the money. He must have—"

He squeezed her knee, and she gritted her teeth.

"No. Your brother has paid me nothing, and I do not believe he will. He has made many false promises—and now he must pay."

"But—but—it would not be him paying, but me. I do not

belong to him. I am married, Laurence will—"

Lord Brett sneered.

"Laurence Walsham is nothing but a womanizing cad. He will not rescue you, and he certainly will not wish to be married to you once you are ruined."

The word ruined sent her blood cold. He couldn't do that to her. Laurence would save her, wouldn't he?

"You didn't want to marry me because you thought Laurence ruined me, so I do not see why I am worth anything to you now."

Brett sneered at her. "I certainly don't want a *wife* who is ruined. If Laurence was foolish enough to end up leg-shackled against his will, then that's his problem. But that does not mean I cannot take you as payment against your brother's debts."

Anger and fear warred within Anastasia. "I am not a commodity that can be used to settle debts," she said, more hotly than was probably advised.

To this, he smirked. "But my dear, you are. Perhaps your brother will pay to have you returned, perhaps Laurence will. Or perhaps I will simply regain the money I have lost in other ways…"

He looked her up and down, and she wanted to be sick.

The coach stopped outside an inn, one which was run-down and in a part of town Anastasia had never been.

"The staff here know not to cross me," Brett said, giving her a warning look. "They will not help you. But I would advise against making a scene—you will only make things worse for yourself."

His voice was cold and menacing and sent a shiver down her spine.

"Laurence will come for me, and you will be sorry," she could not help but say.

But he only laughed. "Laurence married you out of a sense of duty. I'm not sure why you think, now that you're gone, he won't just return to one of his mistresses. He has many, as I'm sure you are aware. He does not need you."

Anastasia shook her head violently. "I will not listen—"

"You do not have to listen to know that it is the truth. Why, only the other day at the Joneses' ball, I saw him closeted away with Lady Frindley. I spoke to her that evening, and she told me all about their long-standing relationship. Why, she seemed awfully enamored with that green waistcoat he was wearing to the ball, and indeed, they left together…"

Anastasia gritted her teeth to stop herself from responding. She did not want to imagine Laurence with another woman, but Brett painted a vivid picture—and she could imagine the very outfit, for she had seen him leaving in it for the ball that she had not attended, the one he had insisted he didn't really wish to go to.

Had she simply been hoodwinked all this time?

Lady Frindley… She had heard that name before, too. Oliver had named her as one of Laurence's mistresses, and here was Brett, naming her again.

Despair washed over her. He would never love her like she loved him. Would never want only her… And now Baron Brett was going to do things to her, ruin her, make her unworthy in the eyes of society and her husband.

She wanted to cry but did not think it would help. And as Baron Brett pushed her roughly from the carriage, she had only one thought: she had to protect the baby.

Perhaps Laurence did not love her, perhaps her life was ruined—but none of that was this child's fault.

# CHAPTER THIRTY-ONE

IT WAS AT least an hour before supper was usually served, but Laurence couldn't find Anastasia anywhere. They had no plans together, and she probably wasn't expecting to see him until the meal was ready, but she wasn't usually hard to find. And yet today, she was not in any of her usual locations, and none of the staff seemed to know where she had gone.

It was rather a mystery.

He wondered, as he glanced into the parlor once more, whether her whereabouts had anything to do with the mysterious visits to the pawnshop—and with her nefarious brother. He had an uneasy feeling in the pit of his stomach, but he told himself to ignore it. He did not tell her everywhere he went, and he had not demanded that she do so either. She would return in time for supper, and he would ask where she had been.

The uncomfortable idea that she was hiding things—that perhaps she was meeting another man—reared its ugly head inside his mind. It was foolish, really; there were many reasons why she might have business that she did not wish to tell him, or did not feel concerned him.

But the damned thoughts kept reappearing and made his skin prickle.

"Are you sure no one knows where Lady Walsham is, Johnson?" he asked for the third time.

Johnson shook his head. "No, my lord. Although Mrs. Yates,

the housekeeper, has just informed me that the maid, Kate, is nowhere to be found either."

At least she was not out alone. If something had happened to her, her maid would be there to fetch help. Although they were probably just paying calls—there was no reason to think something might have gone awry, surely.

"I am sure the girl is with her ladyship, my lord. Although I will ensure in future that she tells someone where they intend to go, to avoid any worry."

Laurence nodded. "Yes, that might be prudent... Although let me speak to Lady Walsham first. It is, of course, her choice whether she informs everyone of her movements. And perhaps she did, and I have just forgotten." He gave a light chuckle, trying to hide his irrational worry from his staff. He knew she had certainly not told him where she was going that afternoon. But he was sure she would soon walk through the door and the whole silly business would be forgotten. He didn't necessarily want the staff reporting on where she was going, but he would speak to her about telling somebody her intended destination, just in case anything went wrong.

Just to stop him worrying about her.

He wanted—nay, needed—to protect her, even if there was nothing to truly protect her from.

There was a commotion at the parlor door, and Johnson frowned, bowing his head to his master before turning to investigate. Laurence's heart was in his throat as he heard the normally staid butler ask in a hurried tone, "Where have you been, Kate? And where is Her Ladyship?"

"She didn't come back," the maid said, her tone bordering on the hysterical. "I waited and waited, but she did not return and—"

Laurence flung the door open and came face to face with the red-eyed maid. "What do you mean, she didn't come back? From where?"

The girl shook where she stood, and looked down at the floor. "I—I—I—"

"I need to know where my wife is," Laurence almost roared; that only made the girl shake more.

"If I may, my lord," Johnson said, in his usual calm tone of voice.

"Yes, yes, of course. My apologies, I just—"

"Perfectly understandable, my lord. Now, Kate, we need to know where you went with Lady Walsham this afternoon. You are not in trouble—we just must ensure she is safe."

The maid nodded and whimpered. "I don't know if Her Ladyship would want me to say," she said in a whisper. Johnson gave Laurence an awkward look, and while Laurence admired the girl's loyalty, he needed to know where his wife was.

"Was it the pawnshop on Cheshire Street?" he asked.

The girl's eyes widened, and she nodded.

"Why would Her Ladyship—" Johnson began, looking at Laurence. And then he seemed to realize—perhaps he saw on Laurence's face—it wasn't his place to ask. "Never mind. Now, you say she didn't come back—did you not go into the establishment with her?"

The maid shook her head. "I—I never do. She asks me to wait in the carriage around the corner, and then she returns. She's never more than half an hour. But today…"

Johnson frowned, as though he found it all highly irregular— and of course, it was. But appearances did not matter now.

"And how long was she this time?" Laurence asked, managing to keep his voice fairly calm.

"I waited nearly two hours, and then I went to the shop myself…but they said she had left a long time ago."

So she had gone back to the pawnshop, and this time, she had not returned. Laurence pulled his hands into fists and tried to think rationally. If only he had confronted her about it, banned her from going, done *something*.

Then perhaps they would not be in this situation—where he did not know where she was, or whether she was safe.

"So she went into the shop at what, around one?"

The maid nodded tearfully.

"So it's been…four hours or so since you last saw her. You can get a fair distance from London in four hours." If they were in the countryside, there would be only one way to go…but from London, there were any number of routes she could have taken.

Had she left him? Was that what was happening? He did not think she had shown any signs that she wanted to leave. They were not some great love match, but he thought they rubbed along together well enough. Sometimes, he had to admit, he did not understand her moods…but there had been no arguments, no moment of upset that he could use to explain why she might have left him.

So where was she? Was she meeting someone else? Or had she been taken against her will?

That was the worst option of all, for although he would have been heartbroken at the thought of her leaving him or having an affair, at least she would be safe. If she had been taken against her will…well, there was no knowing what might've happened to her.

"I must go and speak to her brother," he said, having waded through his thoughts to arrive at a moment of clarity. "He may know something." He did not relish the thought of having to visit Oliver Carrington, but he would do anything to find Anastasia. And perhaps she was there, visiting with her brother.

"If she arrives home, or you hear anything about her whereabouts, send a man to come and get me. You know Carrington's address, yes?"

Johnson nodded. "Of course, my lord. Should we send out the hall boys to look for her?"

Laurence shook his head. "Not yet. There may be a perfectly reasonable explanation for all of this. Let me visit her brother first."

# CHAPTER THIRTY-TWO

ANASTASIA SAT ON the floor in the corner of the sparse chamber and wept. She refused to sit on the bed, knowing exactly how Baron Brett might choose to interpret that when he returned.

She was no fool; she knew the baron could easily overpower her if he wished to. But she wasn't about to make it easy for him. She had only ever lain with one man—her husband—and she did not intend for that to change without a fight.

But she hoped it would not come to that. She hoped, even if he did not love her—even if he had a queue of mistresses lining up to warm his bed—Laurence would rescue her. That he would discover her whereabouts, somehow, and take her away from this hell.

She did not know where Baron Brett had gone. He had been back twice in the hours since he had taken her from the street outside the pawn shop. Well, she thought it had been hours, but her only way of knowing was from the lowering of the sun that she could see through the small window.

There was no way of escaping. She had tried when he had first left, climbing the chair to reach the window, only to realize that it was far too high to escape through without—

Dying.

Death was possibly a fate she would have taken over whatever Baron Brett had in mind, but she would not do that to her unborn child.

And she was still very much hoping for a miracle; hoping that Laurence would burst through the door and save her.

The door was bolted, thick wood that either muffled her cries or at least allowed anyone on the other side to ignore them. And that was it: a chair, a bed, and a locked door. Nothing she could use as a weapon, and nothing she could use to escape.

She heard the key in the door, the metal scraping against the lock. She sat upright, furiously wiping away her tears. She was sure it was obvious that she had been crying, but she wouldn't let him see it. She refused to give him the satisfaction.

He slipped into the room and stood there, watching her from under half-lowered lids. "The hours are ticking by, little one," he said, a smirk on his lips. "It seems you will be my payment, after all."

She did not understand his words. Why did the time passing mean anything? Had he sent a ransom note? And if so, to whom?

Would Laurence receive demands for money and not pay it to retrieve her? She could not truly believe it. Laurence had money, and he was not afraid to spend it.

Oliver, on the other hand? Unfortunately, she now had no confidence that her brother would ever choose her over money. If he had been sent the ransom demand...she did not think he would pay it. But would his pride allow him to go to Laurence?

Or would he just leave his sister as payment?

She shivered at the thought.

LAURENCE HAMMERED ON the Carrington front door, not caring about propriety. When the butler opened the door, he looked a little shocked, perhaps by the expression on Laurence's face.

"I'm afraid Mr. Carrington is presently unavailable," the butler said, a strained expression upon his face.

"I will see him," Laurence growled. "I will charge through this entire house if I have to, or you can lead me to him."

"I cannot—" the butler said, his gaze darting to the closed door of the study, where Laurence presumed Oliver was hiding.

He stepped forward. "Carrington! Come out now, or I will break down every door in this house to find you!"

The butler turned pale; the study door opened.

"Go, James."

The butler hurried away, seeming rather relieved to have been dismissed.

"Where is she?" Laurence did not think that Oliver would have hidden from him had he not known something about Anastasia's disappearance, and so he wasted no time with pleasantries.

"I don't—"

"My wife is missing. Time is of the essence, Carrington. Is she here?"

Oliver shook his head.

"You know where she is." It was not a question.

Oliver shook his head once more. "Not where she is. I know who has her."

Laurence's blood ran cold. So it was the worst of the options: someone had taken her.

"Oh?"

Oliver reached into his pocket and pulled out a piece of parchment, handing it to Laurence.

His eyes dropped straight to the bottom of the missive: Baron Brett. A blight upon their lives yet again.

"How long have you had this?" he asked.

"Not long," Oliver insisted, Laurence's tone—and presence— clearly making him uneasy.

"I believe it was delivered two hours ago, Your Lordship," the butler said, and Oliver's eyes widened with horror as his lie was exposed.

"Two hours?" Laurence took a step towards Oliver. "You

have known *that man* has my wife for two hours and have done *nothing* about it?"

Oliver glared at the butler, who was surely in line to lose his job for his honesty. "Not nothing. I was just getting ready to respond. As you can see, he demands money, and it never does any good to give in to blackmailers."

"He has my *wife*," Laurence roared.

"Unfortunate collateral, yes, but—"

Laurence could not control himself any longer. He took one step closer, and his fist flew, landing squarely on Oliver's weak mouth.

Oliver screamed, recoiled, and clasped his hand to his lip, where blood was already trickling down onto the rug beneath their feet.

"You will tell me what you know, and you will aid me in rescuing your sister—and then you will never darken our doorway again. Do you understand?"

Oliver clasped his lip and did not speak.

Laurence grabbed the man by his cravat and shook him until his teeth chattered. "I said. Do. You. Understand?"

He nodded.

"Good. Now, tell me everything about Brett. What you owe him, what he has said in the past. We need to work out where he is holding her and get her before...before she comes to any harm." Laurence had to close his eyes briefly to fight the wave of nausea that threatened to overwhelm him at the thought of her being hurt or violated. Baron Brett was a vile man, and Laurence did not know the lengths he would go to in order to recoup the money he wanted, or to punish Oliver—although Oliver did not truly seem to care about his sister.

"If he hurts her, I'm holding you personally responsible. I will tear you limb from limb before going on to do the same to him." Anger was a far more productive emotion than the terror he was feeling in the pit of his stomach, and even if it would not make sense to beat Oliver into a pulp right now, he could quite happily

dole out a warning.

They were going to find her, and she was going to be all right. They had to. He couldn't imagine his life without her.

# CHAPTER THIRTY-THREE

DARKNESS HAD FALLEN outside the little window, and Anastasia tried hard not to fall into a pit of despair. Brett came and went, making nasty comments whenever he returned, and she knew soon his patience would run out.

She was rather surprised when he returned with two plates of food and set one before her—although there was no way she could eat. He sat down on the bed and tucked into his meal with a hearty appetite, looking over at her every now and again.

"You should eat. It's late, and we have no idea what the night will bring." He pushed the spoon toward her. There was no way she could think of to use that as a weapon.

She watched him and tried to look for weak spots, tried to plan her attack for when he inevitably followed through on his threats. *I'm sorry*, she told the baby growing within her. *I will keep you safe. I love you.*

Tears sprung to her eyes, and she blinked them away, not wanting to show him any sign of weakness.

But he noticed anyway.

"No need to look so morose. I'm not the devil you've decided I am—merely a man who knows what he wants and will do anything to get it." He finished his mouthful, put his empty plate on the floor at his feet, and wiped his hands down the front of his waistcoat. "Come now."

He stood and approached her, and she shrank back into the

corner, trying to make herself as small as possible. He reached down and plucked her wrist from her lap, roughly pulling her up to stand before him.

She forced herself to look him in the eye. He *was* the devil—she just needed to survive him.

"I've always liked a challenge," he said, and leaned in to give her a rough, unwelcome kiss. The smell of beer and onions on his breath and the feel of his beard against her delicate skin made her want to throw up, and when he pulled away, she almost did.

He reached forward and put a hand on her waist, and she steeled herself to kick him hard where she knew it would hurt. Although what she would do once he was down, she did not know, for the door was locked, and she did not know where the key was.

Perhaps, if she could render him unconscious, she could find it…but she did not know if she was physically capable of doing so.

And then a knock at the door saved her from having to find out whether indeed she could.

Hope bloomed in Anastasia's chest, and her eyes remained fixed on Brett as he covered the short distance between the corner she had been trying to hide in and the door.

He only opened it a crack, yet Anastasia could tell that the man on the other side was not anyone she knew. Was he a friend of Brett? Or someone who might be inclined to help a damsel in distress?

She waited for a moment, listening hard to hear what they were speaking about in hushed tones.

"There's a man downstairs looking for you," she was fairly sure he said.

"No one should know I'm here," Brett replied.

"Well, I don't know how he knows, but he does—and he's damned angry. Threatening to smash the place up. I don't want no trouble, Brett. I don't want the law involved, or my place of business destroyed, you hear me?"

"You've nothing to fear, and besides, I pay you handsomely

for your...*understanding*. Now, let me come and see this gentleman, and get rid of him for you."

Anastasia saw her window of opportunity slamming shut. If whoever the angry man was had come to find her—if it was Oliver, or even better, Laurence—then she couldn't let Baron Brett go down and give them some story about her whereabouts that would lead them to leave her here. She could not be left here. Not with him.

She rushed forward. "Please, help me! I'm being held against my will, this man—" Baron Brett turned, raised his hand, and slapped her clean across the face.

She gasped as the pain overwhelmed her and blinked back tears that had begun to fall unbidden.

"I warned you," Brett said, seemingly unshaken by the entire incident. "Shut your mouth. Now, let me deal with whoever is downstairs causing trouble."

And with that, he closed the door, locking it behind him and leaving Anastasia with her cheek stinging, and tears pouring down her face.


LAURENCE PACED UP and down the bar as he waited for the innkeeper to return. There was something about the shifty look in the man's eye that made him sure Brett was here—no matter what the man said to the contrary.

It hadn't been easy to find this place. After visiting the location of the proposed exchange of money for Anastasia, having worked out the clues in the letter, they then had to threaten and bribe those around to find out where Brett was likely to be.

He knew this was still a long shot, but he would try anything. And when he had threatened to destroy the place, something in his eyes and voice must have rung true, for the man had immediately excused himself—and was hopefully returning with Baron Brett.

Oliver, coward that he was, was waiting outside. Laurence wouldn't have been surprised if he'd left already, but he didn't care. If anything had happened to Anastasia, he would find Oliver, and he would exact his revenge. There was nowhere Oliver could hide to avoid retribution for abandoning the woman that Laurence loved.

The woman he loved. He couldn't unpack the feelings at that moment, for the proprietor returned, with Brett striding behind him.

Laurence balled his hands into fists and reminded himself that if the man was dead, he could not tell him the whereabouts of his wife.

"Where is she?"

"Lord Walsham, what a pleasure to see you," Brett said, a smarmy grin upon his face.

"I've seen the note. I know you have her. Now where is she? Don't mess with me, Brett—I'm not some milksop like Carrington. You *will* regret it."

"If I know the location of your wife—and it really is rather reckless and careless of you to misplace her—then as I made clear in my note, I would only part with such information for a fee."

Laurence gritted his teeth. He would part with any amount of money to see Anastasia safe—and at the same time, he did not wish to give the man a penny. What would stop him from pulling the same stunt again if it worked? And yet he knew he would do anything to get her back, even if it meant giving every penny he had to this man for her safe return. And he could keep Anastasia under surveillance twenty-four hours a day if he had to.

"Give her to me, safe and unharmed, and you can have your money," he spat.

Brett tutted. "This is not the location agreed upon, and if you read the note, you'll know I require the money before any such exchange."

"Goddamn it, Brett, give me my wife."

"You know, I just don't totally believe that you will give me my money. Perhaps you're as fickle as Carrington—never giving me a penny he owes me, even when his sister was pawning her worldly goods—or should I say, *your* worldly goods—to give him the money to do so. Whoops, I hope I haven't got her into trouble."

Laurence didn't care if she pawned every item of value in the house. He just needed to see her safe.

"Give me the money first, and then—"

"Enough!" Laurence roared. Brett was pigheaded and arrogant and didn't seem to fear anybody or anything. But he was not the only person in this inn who knew where Anastasia was—Laurence was sure of it. He turned to the innkeeper, who was pretending to polish glasses while clearly listening to every word that was said.

"You. Have you seen a redheaded woman with this man?"

"I…" He trailed off, looking to Brett for an answer.

"Whatever he's paying you isn't worth what I will do to this place if I do not find my wife. I am not a cruel man, unlike this one—but I will stop at nothing. I will burn the place down, I will make sure you never have another penny to your name, if you are hiding my wife from me. He may be a baron, but I am a viscount—and believe me, I can make your life far more miserable than he can."

For a moment, it looked like the man wasn't going to speak, and his gaze darted to the door as if he wished to run away.

Laurence shook his head. "This is not your fight. Tell me where she is, and I can protect you from him."

The innkeeper swallowed, looked up at Brett, and then said, "Upstairs. Top floor. The attic bedroom."

Laurence didn't need to be told twice. A string of profanities from Brett's mouth rang in his ears, but he was already taking the stairs two at a time, praying to God that Anastasia was unharmed.

# CHAPTER THIRTY-FOUR

"A NASTASIA! ANASTASIA!" HE shouted her name as he ran up the stairs, just in case the innkeeper had lied to him and she was, in fact, in another room. He took the stairs with ease, anger and desperation fueling him until he reached the top of the rickety building and the attic room he had been directed toward.

It had a thick wooden door, which was closed, and he pulled at it, but it did not budge. "Anastasia?"

"Laurence?" Her voice was muffled, but it was unmistakably hers. "Laurence, is that you?"

"I'm here, I'm here," he said, hearing terror in her voice and hating himself for it. He should have found her sooner, should have known she was missing. "I can't get in, I'll have to—"

"He has the key," she said, her voice louder now, as though she had moved closer to the door. "I don't know where he is, but he has it. I can't open it, I've tried—and I think it's too thick to break down."

"I'll get it. Don't worry, you're safe now—I promise."

SHE HEARD HIS footsteps retreating on the other side of the door and had to hold herself together to avoid breaking down into tears. He wasn't abandoning her, surely just going to find the key, but she hated him leaving all the same. She just wanted to get out of this room as soon as possible.

He had come, though. Brett had tried to say he wouldn't, that he didn't care—but he must do, for he had found her, and he was going to rescue her. Did it really matter if there were other women in his bed, if he cared about her? Could she learn to live with it?

If she got out of this room untouched by Baron Brett, save for that disgusting kiss and the slap across the face, she thought she could learn to live with anything.

It didn't take him long to return, and when she heard the key in the lock, her heart jumped for joy—only for the joy to be dampened somewhat by the sight of Baron Brett leering at her on the other side of the door. He was soon shoved aside, however, by Laurence, who barreled into the room and pulled her toward him, holding her tight before pulling her away a little in order to look at her.

"If he's hurt a hair on your head, I swear—" He turned to Baron Brett, a menacing look in his eyes, and Anastasia found herself worrying about what was going to come next. Not that she cared if Brett got hurt—it was more than he deserved. But she didn't want anything to happen to Laurence in the fray.

Laurence reached forward and plucked the key from Baron Brett's hand, and Anastasia's pulse slowed a little, knowing she would not be locked in by that man again.

"She's here of her own accord, Walsham. We've been meeting regularly since you foiled our plan to marry. At the pawnshop on Cheshire Street. You know the one."

Anastasia gasped. The man seemed willing to lie endlessly. "Liar! He abducted me, Laurence, I swear—"

Laurence took her hand in his and squeezed it tightly. "I know he is a liar, my love. I'm only sorry I didn't get here sooner." He turned back to her, and she almost melted at the tender way he looked at her. "Did he touch you? Did he do...anything?"

"He kissed me," she told him, for she did not want there to be any lies between them. Not now. "But nothing else. Nothing...worse."

"Thank God," Laurence muttered under his breath, and then turned to face Brett. "You are not guilty of all the crimes I thought you might be—although I have no doubt you would have acted on your impulses if you had not been stopped."

"You can't try a man for his thoughts," Baron Brett said, surprisingly confident for a man who had been caught abducting a viscountess. "Now, just give me my money, and we can pretend none of this ever happened. No one needs to know that your wife was alone in a bedchamber with me, so there will be no question about the legitimacy of any children she may bear in the year to come."

Anastasia's eyes widened. He could not know she was already with child, could he? She had barely realized it herself, so surely there was no way a man who did not know her well could. But if knowledge of this sorry affair leaked to the ton, would they indeed question whether the child she was carrying—Laurence's child—was in fact an illegitimate by-blow?

But Laurence simply let out a harsh laugh.

"You really are delusional, aren't you? You have committed a serious crime. There will be no money—I will not stop until you have been imprisoned for your terrible deeds."

But the oily smile did not disappear from Brett's face. "You see, I was right. You may be a viscount, but you do not keep your word. Which is why I made sure I had an insurance policy." He pulled a pistol from his coat pocket, and Anastasia screamed. Had he had that all along? She had planned to fight him, and yet he could have put a bullet through her at any moment, had he chosen to. Ended her life...ended her child's life.

It was too much to bear.

"She's worth ten thousand pounds, isn't she?" Brett said, pointing the gun straight at Anastasia. "Or now that she is ruined, her reputation sullied by being with me, do you find you no longer care so much?"

His finger rested lightly on the trigger, and Laurence moved swiftly in front of her, blocking her view of the man, shielding her from the gun.

That didn't make her feel much better. She did not want to die, but she could not lose him. She loved him—she knew that now. She could not lose him like this.

"Don't be foolish, Brett. You shoot me and you'll be hanged as a murderer. You may be vile, but you're not a fool."

"Don't worry, I have many friends on the continent. I can disappear until people have forgotten all about Viscount Walsham." Laurence lifted his arm, perhaps to stop Brett, perhaps to reach out and stop him—and in that moment, Anastasia caught a glimpse of the baron, as he raised the gun and pointed it dead at Laurence's heart.

"Last chance, Walsham. The money, your life, or hers."

The bang of the pistol firing forced Anastasia's eyes shut, and then she screamed and gripped onto Laurence tightly, sure that he was about to crumple before her.

But he did not. He was strong and steadfast, her shield, and when she opened her eyes, she saw the blood-splattered arm of Baron Brett, who had just found his voice and begun to shout a string of profanities as he held tightly to the wound in his arm. In the shock of it all, Brett had dropped the gun, and so Anastasia dared step around Laurence to try to see what on earth was going on.

Brett had not been the only one with a gun. As Laurence bent down to pick up the pistol, Anastasia's eyes widened in shock to see the sight of her brother standing with a gun pointed at Brett, the barrel still smoking from where he had discharged it.

"What have you done?" Brett screamed at the shaking figure of Oliver.

"I couldn't let you shoot my sister," he said, sounding as surprised by that fact as Anastasia was.

"I wasn't going to shoot her, you fool. Simply scare them enough that they handed over the money—money that you owe me, I hasten to remind you. And now look what you've done—you could have shot my arm off."

"You'll live," Laurence said, sounding rather irritated by the fact. "And there are men downstairs with some questions for you; I'm sure they'll make sure you get the appropriate medical care. Once you explain why you had a viscountess locked away up here."

"You didn't say anything about calling the authorities," Oliver said, and Anastasia saw Brett eying the small window, checking it for a chance to escape, just as she had done earlier.

"I was not about to let a man get away with abducting my wife, trying to ransom her, and God knows what else. Besides, the authorities being here ensures I exercised restraint," he added, glaring at Brett. "Not that it is deserved."

"But I just shot a man…" Oliver said, the gun shaking in his hands.

"And in doing so saved all of our lives. Do not fear, Carrington—your good deed will not go unrewarded. I thought you a coward, but it seems I was not entirely correct." Laurence took Anastasia's hand, as though reassuring himself that she was definitely there, and then turned back to Brett. "Now, will you come downstairs quietly, or do Carrington and I need to physically bring you to the magistrate?"

ANASTASIA KEPT IT all together until she stepped inside their carriage and the door closed, and she was alone with Laurence.

And then her teeth began to chatter, her knees began to knock, and a violent sob tore through her.

"You're safe," Laurence said, pulling her toward him and engulfing her in his embrace. "You're safe. I won't ever let anyone hurt you again. You're safe, my love—I promise."

He watched her fall apart in front of him and gathered her

close, wanting to save her from the pain, wanting to make everything all right.

She was here, she was safe, and thankfully Brett had not violated her. They had watched him be taken away by the magistrates, and he had been glad that he had contacted them before arriving at the inn—for he was not sure what he would have done to the man if he had not known that men of the law were downstairs waiting for him. He hadn't been lying when he said their presence had caused him to exercise restraint.

Anastasia pressed her face into his neck and sobbed against him, and he held her close and stroked her back and told her that everything would be all right.

Oliver had been a surprise. He had presumed the man had run off as soon as Laurence was out of sight, but it seemed he did love his sister, somewhere deep down. He had not treated her properly, but perhaps he could still make amends. Perhaps it wasn't too late.

"Let's go home," he said, tapping his knuckles against the roof of the carriage, signaling to the driver to head home.

She did not speak until the carriage stopped once more. She pulled herself away from him, her eyes red and puffy.

"Thank you for saving me. I thought... I thought it was all going to end very differently."

"I'll always be there for you, Anastasia. I..." He so nearly said it. Told her the truth of his heart—that he loved her. That he could not imagine his life without her.

This did not feel like the time. He wanted to get her inside, to calm her down, to help her forget—and then he could tell her. Once this was all a memory.

"I don't want to stay here," she said, holding her head high.

Laurence frowned. "I don't understand. Where do you want to go? Your brother's house?"

Anastasia shook her head. "I don't want to stay in London. I'm sorry, I know you want to, but it just isn't the place for me. I was always happier in the countryside, and I think we could be happier too, away from all this."

His face felt like it would split from the grin he couldn't contain. "We'll leave tomorrow, if that's what you want. It's too late tonight."

Her eyes began to water again. "Really? It's that easy? You don't mind?"

Laurence took her hands in his. "I'd do anything for you, Anastasia. And if I'm honest, I've only stayed in London this long because I thought it was what you wanted. I'd rather be in the countryside."

# CHAPTER THIRTY-FIVE

WHEN SHE WOKE up, it took Anastasia a few moments to realize where she was. She recognized the arms wrapped around her and relaxed into Laurence's warm embrace, feeling safe with him so close.

But the room was one she had never slept in before: Laurence's room. They had always slept together in her bedchamber, with him leaving to return to his own room in the beginning. But he had never brought her here.

She barely remembered arriving home, though she vaguely recalled him carrying her from the carriage and up the stairs. She supposed his room was closer, and so it made sense for them to sleep there.

As he slumbered, her mind wandered back to the events of the previous day: the fear she had felt, the horror at what Brett might do, and the fact that it had been Oliver, in the end, who had saved them both from him.

She couldn't forgive Oliver for everything he had done...but perhaps they could start again. Perhaps the brother she had seen glimpses of over the years—the brother she loved—was still there.

She wanted to look at Laurence's face, but she didn't dare move in case she woke him. She brought it to mind easily anyway: his rich brown eyes, his thick, dark hair. He had risked his life for her, and her heart felt full in the knowledge that however they had begun, he did care for her. Her hand moved to her stomach. And he would care for their child, she was sure.

"Good morning," he said in a low, raspy voice, then cleared his throat before pressing a kiss to her shoulder. "Have you been awake long?"

She shook her head and wriggled in his arms until she was facing him.

"Not long. Although I was a little confused about where I was…"

Concern furrowed his brow. "Perhaps you would have preferred to sleep alone, in your own chamber. I was not very thoughtful—"

"This is where I want to be. I've just never slept here before." She ran a finger down the bridge of his nose, easing away the frown line on his forehead. "Can we really leave for the countryside today?"

He smiled at her and nodded. "Of course. You should have told me you didn't want to stay in the city."

She cocked her head to one side and smiled at him ruefully. "So should you."

"That's true, I suppose. And while we're on the topic of things we *should* have said…"

Anastasia's heart leapt into her throat. What did he need to tell her that he hadn't already? She felt happy and safe and content in the knowledge that they were to move to the countryside, where they would have this child—and hopefully many more. She only hoped he would not have something to say that would ruin it all.

"Anastasia, I should have told you this before, but I don't quite know when I realized it. I love you. I would do anything to make you happy. Anything at all. I am yours—heart, body, and soul."

Joy overwhelmed her, and for a moment she could not speak. He loved her. He loved her—and he would do anything for her.

"I love you too," she finally managed to choke out, and the

surprise on his face almost made her laugh. She had thought that the feelings growing inside her must have been plain on her face, but apparently not. Before she could repeat the words, he pressed his lips to hers and kissed her until she was breathless.

"We can start again, Anastasia. Start in the countryside with a marriage based on love and trust and honesty."

Anastasia ducked her head. "I'm sorry I lied to you. About the pawnshop, about the money..."

"It doesn't matter now. But in future, I want us not to hide things, not to be quiet about what will make us happy. Like living in the countryside, like..."

Anastasia took a deep breath. "I am happy, Laurence. Happier than you could ever know, knowing that you feel the same way I do about you. But there has been one thing bothering me..."

"Then tell me, my love, because I don't want anything to upset you."

Her face grew red at the words she must speak—but he was right. They could start again, with a marriage based on love and honesty. She didn't need to worry about where he was or how he felt.

"I know before we were married, you had a certain...reputation. And when we were not in love, our marriage perhaps did not preclude... But maybe now, in the countryside, it will be easier..."

Laurence frowned. "I'm lost. I don't understand what you're saying."

Anastasia swallowed and forced the words out. "I would be happier if...if you no longer had any mistresses. If it was just me and you." She felt like she was asking too much, like no one could ever care so much for her as to promise to be faithful and true. But he had said he loved her, and he had said he would do anything.

And that was all she wanted.

He laughed, and the sting of it made her pull back slightly, putting some space between them. If he said no, it would hurt—

but laughing at her wishes? That was almost worse.

"If you cannot—"

"No, it's not that. Anastasia—I may not have been in love with you from the day we wed. But I have been faithful. There has been no other woman but you since I put that ring on your finger, and I promise there will be no one else while you walk this earth."

⇜⇝

ALL THIS TIME she had thought he was seeing other women—when in fact, he had only wanted her. One request, and it was so simple for him to fulfill. It almost didn't seem fair that he should get such happiness without paying a greater price.

"While we are being honest with one another," Anastasia said, biting her bottom lip.

Laurence's heart began to pound. What did she need to tell him that he didn't already know? They had found such happiness, that it seemed terrifying to him to risk it.

And yet he wanted honesty, just as he wanted love.

She reached out and took his hands and placed one upon her belly. "I am carrying your child."

His eyes widened, and his hand did not move from the slight curve of her stomach. "Are you sure?" he asked.

"As sure as I can be. It is not something I know an awful lot about. But I have not... I have not bled now in three months."

"We're to have a baby," he said, the smile growing upon his face.

"I know how important it is for you to have an heir, but of course I do not know whether this will be a boy... But if it is not, we can try again, and..."

He took her hands in his and pressed them to his lips. "Anastasia. Anastasia. I will love our child whether it is a son or a daughter. I promise you that. Yes, I need an heir—but more than that, I need you. I never expected to want a wife, even if I needed one—but now I know you are the wife I needed all along, because I want you. Here in London, in the country, in my bed, in yours, in every aspect of my life—for as long as we both shall live. And however many children we are given, I will love them equally. I will love them, and you, with all my heart."

# EPILOGUE

*Two Years Later*

"I T'S SUCH A beautiful day," Laurence said, as they sat and ate breakfast together in the dining room at Longberry House. They had retreated there the day after the terrible abduction that Anastasia had suffered, and save for occasional nights visiting friends, they had not left.

Neither of them wished to be back in London, and neither of them wished to be away from their little family.

Their little but growing family.

"I thought we might take a picnic into the meadow for lunch, if you're not too tired to walk there."

Anastasia shook her head and rubbed a hand across her burgeoning belly. "I may be slow, but I can manage that distance. It sounds like a lovely idea—and Jonathan could play in the stream since it's so sunny."

Little Jonathan, who was approaching his second birthday, clapped his hands delightedly at the prospect. Laurence and Anastasia both beamed at him, and then at one another.

Even now, her breath caught a bit when she looked at her handsome husband.

The days at Longberry House were long and languid and full of joy. Laurence tended to matters of business when he had to, and Anastasia was the patron of a local charity, which supported motherless girls to find their way in life. Without a female role model, Anastasia had always felt she had no one to turn to, so the charity seemed a perfect fit.

But the three of them were happiest when they spent time together—not as the Viscount and Viscountess Walsham, but just as a happy family, riding across the countryside when Anastasia was able, teaching Jonty how to skim stones across the lake, or taking picnics out in the meadow, like Laurence had suggested today.

They walked slowly, the picnic basket hooked over Laurence's arm, Jonty holding each of their hands between them. Anastasia's time was only a few weeks away, and she swore she had grown far bigger with this child than she had with her first. Perhaps one simply forgot the trials and tribulations of pregnancy once it was over. She certainly had no wish to recall childbirth—not until she had to. But she sometimes found herself imagining what this next child would be like. Jonathan was the spitting image of his father—dark-haired, dark-eyed, with a handsome smile that no one was capable of saying "no" to. She wondered if this next babe would favor her, or whether there would be another mini Laurence running around.

Her red hair had always been both a source of pride and of frustration. She rather liked that the hue was so different from everyone else's locks; but she had certainly been teased because of it, even by her brother, who had the same reddish tint.

"Swing!" Little Jonty cried, and he giggled maniacally as his mother and father counted to three and then swung him through the air, his laughter echoing throughout the meadow.

Although the walk was not particularly long at all, Jonty's legs were only short, and soon he was crying and holding his arms aloft to both his parents.

"Come here, little man," Laurence said, swinging the boy up into his arms and onto his shoulders. "You're getting too heavy for Mama, but it'll be a long time before Papa can't lift you."

Their son giggled melodically as his father pretended to be a horse and clip-clopped through the trees, the basket still swinging on his arm, seemingly unfazed by the weight of the child and the picnic.

Anastasia rubbed circles against her stomach as the child within her kicked, not wanting to be left out of the family scene. Her heart felt full. She had loved her own father dearly, and Laurence had loved his—and now their child adored him just as much.

She only hoped that Jonty would have a more cordial relationship with his little brother or sister than Anastasia had had with her older brother. Oliver had begun to redeem himself after saving her from the gun of Lord Brett, but they would never again be close. She had spent years trusting him when he ought not to have been trusted, and she did not think she could ever put faith in him again.

She rested a hand on her abdomen, with a sigh. She only hoped that history would not repeat itself. But Jonty was such a kind, sweet-natured little lad—she could not imagine him turning out like Oliver.

"Is all well?" Laurence asked, turning around and smiling broadly at her. "Is that daughter of mine giving you great trouble?" Somewhere along the way, he had become convinced that she was carrying a girl, and she smiled every time he referred to the babe as his daughter, hoping he would not be disappointed if he was wrong and they had another son.

Although, she thought it very likely that a third child would join them in the not-too-distant future. After all, they were more in love than ever, and her fertility had thus far not seemed to be an issue.

"I was just thinking about the future," she said, catching up to her husband and son. "About Jonty, and this baby—"

"His little sister," Laurence said confidently.

Anastasia laughed. "I just hope that they can have a better relationship than I had with my brother, or your father had with your uncle." After all, the only reason Laurence had wanted to marry was because his father had been desperate for him to have an heir, so that his younger brother—a wastrel by all accounts— would never have a chance to inherit.

Well, his wish had been fulfilled. One day—although Anastasia did not like to think on it too closely—Jonty would be the viscount. And his sons after him. Though hopefully, he would never feel so strongly about a younger brother inheriting that he would start making his own sons vow to wed.

Although that had all worked out rather well—for both Laurence and Anastasia. For if Laurence had not been convinced of the need to produce an heir, to honor his father's last wishes, would he have proposed marriage after they were caught speaking on the dark walk of Vauxhall Gardens?

"We will teach both our children—" Laurence paused. "*All* of our children," he added with a laugh, "how important it is to love their siblings, and to stand up for them—even if they fall out, even if they're annoying, even if they disagree. We'll be united as one family, I promise you—no matter how many children we have."

"I love you," she said, delighting in saying the words out loud even after all this time.

"And I love you," Laurence said, bending to place a kiss on her lips, Jonty laughing in his position above them on his father's shoulders.

"And we love you too, little man," Anastasia said, reaching up to ruffle his dark locks before Laurence stood fully, lifting him out of her reach.

"And our little girl," Laurence said, placing a hand to her stomach.

"Of course," Anastasia said, not bothering to argue with him about the possibility of her carrying another boy.

They found a spot by the stream and Laurence gave into Jonty's pleading to play in the babbling water, and Anastasia watched them, a hand upon the life stirring within her, and marveled at how her heart had found room for so much love. She wasn't completely alone anymore; her life—and her heart—were full of people she loved, and who she knew beyond any doubt loved her just as much.

# About the Author

Daphne Quinn loves nothing more than curling up with a large cup of tea and a regency romance. She adores the drama and the dresses of the past—even though she is quite happy with all the comforts of the present! She loves living in England and visiting historic sites like the beautiful city of Bath. She shares photos of her visits—as well as upcoming releases and sales!—on her Facebook page facebook.com/authordaphnequinn.

www.ingramcontent.com/pod-product-compliance
Lightning Source LLC
Chambersburg PA
CBHW072133300726
48975CB00003B/1039

9 781969 349560